Phases of
a Broken Sky

Cursed Moon Series Book One

Christina L. Barr

Table of Contents

Chapter One 5

Chapter Two 19

Chapter Three 33

Chapter Four 41

Chapter Five 49

Chapter Six 63

Chapter Seven 71

Chapter Eight 81

Chapter Nine 93

Chapter Ten 103

Chapter Eleven 109

Chapter Twelve 131

Chapter Thirteen 139

Dear Reader, ... 147

Chapter One

Change.

Most people hate it. I think it mostly has to do with embracing a phobia. Well, I don't know who would "embrace" a phobia unless you wanted attention or something, but fear of change is real. I think my parents were afraid of losing me, and it was a legitimate fear they had experience with. When I was little, I had a brother who died in a tragic car accident. A neighbor was backing out of their driveway like a lunatic and didn't see that Kevin had wandered next door to pick up a runaway soccer ball. No matter how much they love me, they never really got over him. I was their only baby left, and they were suffocating me with their kisses and hugs. It was going to kill them if they finally gave me a chance to breathe.

Then, there was the fear of the unknown. I was afraid of what might be different. My parents had a therapist who told them some distance from me was healthy, but they didn't really listen to that advice. You'd think, after how much they paid for those sessions, that they'd listen to the doctor. Instead, they followed me wherever I went.

You know how a child cries after their mom and dad leave them stranded on their first day of kindergarten? Well, that was my mom's role to play. She was the one crying, and she had a heck of a time convincing me I wanted to be homeschooled, and it worked. They were my friends, and they were my perfect caretakers. Mom insisted on doing everything, so I barely knew how to make a bowl of pasta without the noodles becoming too soft. I was legitimately afraid of not being able to take care of myself, so I had to leave. The baby bird had to jump. Whether it was suicidal or brave, was yet to be discovered.

"Are you sure you wanna do this?" Mom asked. She was clutching onto my car keys so tight, I didn't know if she was gonna hand them over or not.

"Of course, I am, Mom. I've already been accepted. It's been paid for. I wanna be a doctor."

Dad stopped putting luggage in the car for the hundredth time that morning. I swear, he was moving slow on purpose. "But there are so many reputable schools here. You don't have to go all the way out to Phoenix."

They were right about that. I was honestly only going so far because I felt like I needed to rip the bandage off. If I didn't experience adulthood alone, I wasn't going to have a healthy relationship with anyone. The closest thing to a boyfriend I ever had was a Mormon boy pen pal. My parents wouldn't let me video chat with him. Mom was afraid someone would hack into a webcam if I got one.

"You won't even miss me. I'll call. We can email. I finally got a smartphone yesterday, so we can video chat if you guys decide to break out of the flip phone era with me."

"And we'll be able to track you with GPS?" Dad asked.

"If I decided to enable that feature, yes…" I didn't initiate change often, because they would make me feel all guilty with their big, brown puppy eyes. They must have guilt-faced each other into falling in love, and they made sure to never show me their technique.

"I'm gonna call. A lot. There's no reason to be so concerned about me."

"You're driving across the country!" Mom said.

"We should drive you," Dad said adamantly for the billionth time. "I mean it this time—"

"You meant it every other time, and I still refuse to let you. I can do this!" I was desperate for everyone to believe that, including myself. "I know the rules of the road. I won't speed. I won't drive when I'm too tired. I won't—"

"Pick up hitchhikers?"

My mouth dropped. "Dad, I'm not an idiot. I won't tell anyone I'm driving alone. I'll only stop to pee, eat, and rest. I will be responsible."

They were staring at me with the guilt look again. I had to be strong, so I walked in the house, grabbed my last box sitting by the door, and packed it into the back of the already stuffed SUV. I had made my mind up, and nobody was gonna stop me. If they wanted to follow me, that was their business, but I wasn't letting anyone else into that car.

Mom threw her head back and grunted. "Fine! You win." She handed me my keys.

"She wins?" Dad squealed. "You want her to win this?"

"She's not giving us much of a choice, sweetheart." Mom went inside the house and grabbed a camera waiting near the door. "One more memory before the road?"

"Nobody uses those things anymore, Mom. My generation takes selfies."

"Selfies?" Dad asked. "That sounds incredibly vain."

"That sums up my generation quite well, actually." I stood in front of them and held my phone up in the air. "Make a duck face or something."

Mom and Dad tried, but they looked ridiculous. I broke my composure and laughed at them as the photo snapped. I loved it to pieces. "I'll email this to you guys and post it online."

"Online?" Mom shrieked. "Just be careful about college. Okay? It starts off innocent with these selfies; someone posts a picture of you in your bikini, and then, you start posting pictures in your underwear. Next thing you know, you're experimenting with your sexuality with some kinky senior."

"Mom, be serious. That is not everyone's college experience, and it certainly won't be mine." I experienced puberty locked in my house. I didn't even have a boy band poster up in my room. My biggest crush growing up was John Smith, and that might have mostly been because Mel Gibson's voice was so dreamy.

"I'm lame. I was born lame. I'll die lame. Lame. Lame. Lame."

"You are not lame!" Dad kissed me on my forehead. "You are my special little star."

"Yeah, and that doesn't make me feel any less lame…" I hugged him and Mom one final time before jumping into my car. I couldn't believe I had one to my name. It was the most normal thing they could have done for me. Maybe they subconsciously knew I had to escape.

"Be safe."

"I promise." I waved to them as they hugged each other for a source of comfort. It was time to journey on to the rest of my life. Hopefully, I wouldn't be a homeschooled freak incapable of making friends. All my life, I wanted to experience what it felt like to be normal. Going to college across the country, and away from my protective parents, seemed like a step in the right direction.

As I backed out of the driveway and shifted gears, the fear started to leave. Change wasn't always about fear. It was exciting too. I wanted to experience things I never had before. I wanted to take risks, stay up late, and eat junk food. I wanted to meet interesting people and fall in love. I was a young adult. It was time for me to step out and shine like the bright star my dad always claimed I was.

…and I still sounded so lame.

I entered a route in my GPS that avoided toll roads. It didn't make my trip much longer, so I figured there was no harm done. I ended up taking a weird trip across the state. It was deep into the boonies where the tourist attractions were mini golf, and odd statues of bears roamed the land. I was starting to feel sort of uncomfortable with my choice to avoid tolls, but I had never been anywhere. I didn't know whether road trips were supposed to be so…desolate.

A couple of hours into driving, and I was already very bored. My list of parentally approved songs was very short, so I turned the internet radio on through my phone for a little while. I found a new song or two to like, but I realized music wasn't going to help. I had never driven a long distance by myself, and I wanted someone to talk to.

I thought about calling my parents, but I nipped that idea in the bud real fast. I couldn't depend on them forever, and they had to get used to the idea of not seeing or hearing from me for a while. Two hours was not a long enough separation. Besides, I was an only child. I was used to being alone. I should have been able to deal.

It probably wouldn't have been so bad if I didn't feel like I was so out in nowhere. It was creepy! There were no signs of life anywhere, and all the restaurants were literally named "restaurant." If some country hick threatened to chop me up into little pieces, I would tell the police the most generic name ever, and they wouldn't be able to figure out where my remains were. My parents would have me on the missing persons list forever. They wouldn't be able to bear another funeral for a child.

I eventually saw a sign of life walking down the side of the road about two hours later. I didn't see a busted-up car lit on fire or anything drastic like that. I couldn't see the man's face, but he had on a worn brown leather jacket and a grey hoodie covering his face. The closer I got, I saw he was holding out his arm, and his thumb was straight up in the air.

Maybe this was rude of me, but I laughed. There was no way anyone was going to pick up a hitchhiker! I sure wasn't going to. Maybe he would've had a chance if we didn't live in a world where every bad thing was reported on thousands of social media outlets, and sickos didn't maximize them in horror movies all the time. Everyone knew not to do it.

"Poor guy." I shook my head. I felt bad for him if he genuinely needed help. I was a good person, but self-preservation was important to me. My parents would have murdered me if I had even asked them for permission. I couldn't do something that stupid.

I kept driving with my smug face on. Then, karma smacked me right in my face. I reached down to look at my phone—so I could skip a song I didn't like—and by the time I looked up, my front right tire was running over some barbed wire in the road. It was just my awful luck that it wrapped around my tires. I gripped the wheel as the car shook and directed it to the side of the road. Even though no one was coming, I checked the road at least three times before I jumped out to assess the damage.

There were plenty of holes. I couldn't patch up the tire, and I wouldn't know how to anyway. My first thought was to call my dad, but he would have driven all the way out to help me. I didn't want him to do that, and I didn't wanna wait all that time. I called a roadside assistance company, but they quoted me four hours! I didn't want to wait that long either.

I knew there had to be a spare tire. I mean, all cars have them. They're always there in the movies. I didn't have a clue how to change my tire, and I probably should have learned how to do it before I decided to drive across the country. It was a little too late to mull that poor choice over, though.

I moved some of my boxes and luggage out of the back, so I could get to the compartment in the trunk area. There was, indeed, a tire under the floor and a bag with tools inside. There was a jack (I guess), a tire iron, and some kind of hook thingy. The tire was heavy, but I managed to get it out without it completely tackling me to the ground.

I tried to watch a video on how to change my tire, but my 4G was lousy in that area. There was no way I'd be able to watch a video without it buffering constantly. I figured I was a smart enough girl to explore my way to a solution. Obviously, I had to remove the tire. The tire iron was for that. I knew about "righty tighty, lefty loosey." I tried to move the nuts, but I couldn't get the tire iron to budge. I tried kicking it, but it still wouldn't move.

I knew I'd at least have to raise the car, so I got the jack out and put it under the car near the tire. I figured any place was good. I carefully observed the thingy with the hook and realized it was a lever. But when I tried to raise the jack, it wouldn't move. "No way!" I tried pumping it several different times, but I—apparently—had a defective jack.

I probably should have called my dad at that point, but I knew I would need a jack, and I needed to remove my tire. He wouldn't be able to talk me through things I couldn't do. I plopped into the grass and decided to wait for roadside assistance.

I was in a messed-up situation, but I wasn't scared. I was frustrated that I was so ill-prepared. But if I could get through that little scrape without my parents coming to my rescue, then maybe the unknown world of being an adult wouldn't be so scary after all.

Ten minutes into waiting, I looked up the road and saw a figure walking toward me. "Crap! It's the hitchhiker." I felt terrified. I drove right past him, and God struck me down with instant karma. Maybe it wasn't karma. Maybe he was some kind of evil witch doctor, and he cursed my car. But even if it were an honest coincidence, he was probably going to cave my head in with a rock and steal my car if I didn't do something!

I rushed to put my things back in the car. I didn't want him to see my box of Beanie Babies or pictures of my family. I was at the beginning of a horror movie, or what I imagined the beginning of them to be like. I moved so fast; I didn't put the spare tire back in, but I was running out of time. I jumped into the middle seat and locked the car.

"What am I doing?" I had no idea why I was hiding. I didn't want him to know I was there, but I didn't want him to think I had abandoned my car. Besides, I was just lying down flat. He could look inside and see me.

I sat up and waited impatiently. Perhaps he would just pass right by me. He couldn't hitchhike in a broken car anyway. He wouldn't bother me. No, he wouldn't. I was sure of it.

"Hello?"

"Ahhh!" I felt like such a dork. I don't know why I screamed. I knew he was coming. I saw him out of the corner of my eye, and I still jumped like a little baby.

"Are you having some car trouble?" He had a bit of a southern drawl, but it wasn't obvious. I think I only recognized it because my parents liked to watch an old TV show about oil in Texas.

I slowly looked to my right to see him. He had a bit of a beard. It wasn't duck hunter bushy. It was enough that I could see the shape of his masculine face. He still had his hoodie up, but he had long hair, like he walked off the set of a manly shampoo commercial in a shed or something.

I turned my head from him. Just because he was a young man who might have been attractive didn't mean he wouldn't drag me to that shampoo set and bathe in my blood. I couldn't trust him.

"I can fix your tire for you."

I was determined to remain firm, but I could feel the water bottle I chugged beginning to claim its vengeance upon me. I was not going to pee in my car. I scooted over to the door and rolled down my window slightly. "Hi."

"Hi…" His brows cocked like I was a freak, but I did get a chance to see into his eyes. They were pretty hazel, and it occurred to me I hadn't really been that close to a boy alone before, and I scooted away again.

"Why would you help me fix my tire?"

"Because I'm a Good Samaritan."

"Or maybe you wanna eat me…" I mumbled.

"I don't eat people. At least, I haven't yet…" He chuckled lightly and with a twinge of nervousness.

"I don't wanna be your first people snack!"

He chuckled again but composed himself. "Look, I'm trying to help you, so you can go on your way. These parts are dangerous, and I don't want you stranded here."

"I called for assistance."

"In an area like this? Good luck with that."

The time quoted was outrageous. "Fine. You can fix my tire."

He slightly glared at me. "Your gratitude overwhelms me."

I rolled up my window and took a deep breath. I could believe there were kind strangers on our planet. It wasn't the smartest thing in the world, but there were times when I would see people get out of their car after an accident, to see if they were alright. Maybe he was a good guy.

I walked around the car and stood away from him. A healthy distance was good. He picked up the tire iron and placed it on one of the bolts. "Those are stuck. I couldn't get them off..."

He turned the tire iron like it was a doorknob. When the bolt came off, he smirked and held it up to brag. "That was pretty easy."

My mouth dropped. I knew I wasn't that strong, but I put my body weight into it. How could it be so easy for him? But I couldn't let him know exactly how amazed I was with him. "You're stronger than me. Big deal!"

He continued working on the other bolts, and they easily came off as well. It was like the universe was watching the world pull a massive prank on me. He kept looking behind me to see my amazed reactions. "Do you have to pee?"

It was really bad now. "Why do you ask that?"

"Because you're shuffling like a child."

I guess I was moving around a lot. "I can hold it."

He looked around. There was no place of business for miles. No other cars were driving down the road. He finally pointed to a spot about fifty feet away. "There are some tall bushes over there. You should go handle your business."

My mouth dropped again, but I gasped in utter appall. "So, you can sneak up on me and drag me back to wherever you came from? Hang me up by my intestines? Sacrifice me to some pagan god?"

He dropped the tire iron and came up on me so fast, I'd be dead or worse if he wanted. "What kind of twisted imagination do you have?"

I was trying not to be super intimidated, but he was quite tall and...masculine. He was junior lumberjack big. I didn't know what sort of words were appropriate to say, but I couldn't stop talking. "My parents watch those investigative programs. I know what creeps do. At the least, you could try to steal my car or my things."

"I certainly wouldn't take your lady clothes, and you can take your keys with you to the bush."

"You probably know how to hotwire a car."

"I do, but I have to fix your tire first."

"Well, then—"

"Are you seriously going to keep insulting me, or are you going to let me fix your tire so you can never see me again?"

I gulped. I wanted to swallow all the other fears in my head and just be grateful. "Thank you."

I went back in my car. I had a duffle bag that contained a roll of toilet paper, some hand wipes, and I grabbed a black plastic bag to put my disposables in. When the hitchhiker saw I was carrying supplies, he laughed. "You carry a roll of toilet paper wherever you go?"

I blushed, but I wouldn't allow myself to be too embarrassed. "My mom went overseas. She went to pee inside the mall, and there was no toilet paper. In the mall! She warned me to never make that same mistake."

"Fair enough."

The tire was ready to be removed, but he had to lift the car to put it on. I couldn't be that dense to be using the jack wrong. "The jack doesn't work, so I don't know how you'll fix it—"

"I'll get it."

"I don't understand how—"

"Go pee!"

He certainly was bossy, but he was older. I felt like I was with my parents again. But I did listen and walked down to the bush. I did really have to go.

I felt gross for peeing out in the open. I checked like twenty times to make sure no one was watching me. I wasn't a master squatter, so I ended up taking off my shoes, pants, and underwear. If my mother knew what I was doing, she would have wept for raising such a wild child. I was walking back to the car with my head hanging low, but I was amazed once I saw my spare tire properly applied.

"How did you do that?" I ran to him, but he stepped away before I could touch him. "I had sanitary wipes and hand sanitizer. I'm cleaner than you."

"I know how to use a car jack."

"It couldn't have been that hard…" I picked up the jack and the lever thingy on the ground. I tried to get it to work, but it wouldn't move for whatever reason. It was stuck. "You've gotta show me what you did."

"I lifted the car myself."

I glared a little bit at him. I didn't enjoy being made fun of. "What do I do with the busted tire?"

"Put it inside the car. You shouldn't drive more than seventy miles on the spare, so you need to find a tire shop and replace it."

I sighed heavily. I didn't expect an expense like a new tire, and now I was off schedule. My parents were going to flip out when I told them what happened. "It has all of that barbed wire on it, though."

"Fine." He picked up the tire from the rim and hurled it back behind the bush where I used the bathroom. "Out of sight, out of mind."

I was amazed by his strength. I didn't know how cut he was, but he was very solid. I wasn't used to seeing the sort of men described in books. He was no Prince Charming. The Huntsman suited him better. "Thank you for your help."

"You're welcome."

It got awkward. I couldn't invite him into my car. I didn't know anything about him, including his name. I didn't wanna ask because I'd have this emotional connection, and I'd always wonder how I could be cruel enough to leave him on the side of the road.

"Well, I should get going."

"You should."

It was even worse because he didn't ask. He helped me, out of the kindness of his heart, even though I was a huge jerk to him for not stopping. I probably wasn't the only car he was gonna see all day, but no one else was gonna stop, and I at least knew he was an upstanding citizen.

"Goodbye." I reached out for an awkward handshake. He grinned hard, and I did as well, but he wouldn't take my hand. I was shaming myself in my head as I walked to the driver's side and got in. I dealt with an emotional dilemma for sixty seconds before I started the car.

He had no hope in me changing my mind. He started walking, and he never even looked back at me with sympathetic eyes. I think that made it all worse.

"I hope I don't regret this." I drove ahead of him, stopped the car, and rolled down the passenger window. "Get in."

He stopped and turned to me with a cocked brow. "Are you insane?"

"No…" I was highly confused, though. I was certain that gratitude was supposed to follow. "I'm trying to do the right thing here."

"I'm a grown man. You're a little girl."

"I am adequately grown. I am eighteen years old!"

"And yet, you don't have enough sense to know you don't pick up hitchhikers."

"If that's how you feel, then why are you hitchhiking?"

"Because I need a ride, obviously."

"Then are you just gonna continually insult me, or are you gonna get inside?" I knew what I offered was insane, but he insulted me, and my brain was all sorts of confused. But the truth was that I owed him one. He might have been a little tough, but I didn't think he was gonna trap me in the country and kill me. "I'm not afraid of you."

"You should be." He was strong. Even if he didn't toss that tire, it was something I could sense as well. He could snap me into pieces without even trying. If I had to run for my life from him, I would never make it. You know, when you see a big, scary dog without a leash, and there's this one second that you stare each other down and know you're totally outmatched? All you can do is run, and unless there's a miracle that saves you, you know you're getting bit? That's kind of what I felt like when I stared into his primal and, yet, very captivating eyes.

But I did sense something else. I know it sounds stupid, especially since I just met him, but I could sense he had a strong heart, too. It was kind of like if I could trust him, it would be for forever. He'd be loyal. "I don't buy it. Get in."

He rolled his eyes, but he didn't have anywhere else to go. He opened the side door, tossed his backpack in, and sat next to me. "Just take me as far west as you can."

I felt a chill. It was a really weird coincidence. "I'm actually headed to Phoenix."

I think I broke his brain because he looked baffled. "I need to get to Kansas."

It was weird that we were up so far north in Michigan, and we were headed out so far west. It was crazy that he wanted to hitchhike, just like it was crazy for me to drive. Either he was a Grim Reaper ready to strike me down, or there was some kind of Fate intertwining us.

Or…I was still being totally and completely lame. "I need to sleep eventually, so I'm gonna stop tonight somewhere. I guess I'll let you out then?"

He nodded and faced the window. "We'll figure it out."

"Yeah!" I grabbed my phone and leaned over next to him real quick. I snapped a photo of us together. I was grinning like an idiot, but he was awkward, very annoyed, and pale.

He pushed himself as close to the door as possible. "What are you doing?"

"It's not safe to drive with you, but I totally don't wanna call my parents and tell them I picked up a hitchhiker. They would kill me. I'm gonna buy us some time and post this to social media, so the rest of the world will know if my body ends up mutilated somewhere, they'll know when it happened, where I was, and who I was with."

"That's the dumbest thing you could have said."

"Really, Mr. Grownup?" I posted our picture online, and the facial recognition software was so good that a list of photos popped up suggesting who he might have been. I picked the one that looked the most accurate. "Maxwell Harvey, huh?"

He tried to snatch my phone, but I pulled it away. "I'm trying to be incognito."

"Why? Did you kill someone?"

"No."

"Good, because I'm not trying to die." I skimmed through his profile. He hadn't been online for almost a month. His hometown was in Austin, but he was currently staying in Kansas. He had a Master's in Animation, of all things, and he was twenty-four. "You're not that much older than me."

"I'm old enough."

I logged out of my profile and put a lock on my phone. We were bound together by the internet. It was a done deal. "My name is Jesse Holloway, by the way."

"I know."

I got that creepy chill thing again. "How do you know?"

He reached in the back seat and picked up a blue jean jacket that had my first name bedazzled into it with rhinestones. "Grownups do this all the time."

I could have been embarrassed, but I pursed my lips and owned it like a rock star. "You bet, they do."

So, I did the very thing my parents told me not to do. I hoped he didn't turn out to be a psycho killer, because I really didn't want to die. But it was kind of exciting. It was so unlike me to take such a risk, and I didn't question it too much. Little did I know—at the time—there was something drawing us together, or rather, me to him.

Chapter Two

It was odd driving with a perfect stranger in my car. He must have thought it was weird. He probably wasn't intimidated by me. He seemed like he was upset about something, though. The color hadn't returned to his face, and he was still breathing in and out heavily like he had run a mile and didn't want me to know about it.

"So, how did you get here? More importantly, how did you get up here abandoned?"

He took a couple of seconds before he was calm enough to answer. "I was doing some research in the U.P."

"Oh my gosh! I've never been to the Upper Peninsula." I was supposed to go with my parents, but something always sort of came up. "Was it gorgeous?"

"But you're from Michigan?" he laughed. "You've never crossed the bridge or seen Mackinac Island?"

"Well, you're from Texas and Kansas. Have you ever drilled for oil or got swept up in a tornado?"

"No. Of course not."

"Then all my hopes and dreams for you are long gone now." I didn't mean to be snippy, but he rubbed me in a weird way.

But he showed me a tiny smile, so he must have enjoyed rubbing me...Or I must have enjoyed the way he rubbed me the wrong...way...

"It was beautiful up there, but I didn't exactly have time to enjoy it. I didn't find what I was looking for."

"And what were you looking for?"

"We don't know each other well enough for that conversation."

The fact that he wouldn't say made me nervous. I was worried he was a psychotic killer. It was very possible he would chop me into little goldfish bits. "Can you at least tell me why you're hitchhiking? I assume you must have flown here."

"I was robbed."

"Oh. That's messed up." I glanced over to him. I couldn't be sure under his jacket and hoodie, but I was fairly certain he was cut. Plus, he threw that tire far. "You seem like the sort of guy who can take care of himself."

"I usually can, but I was outnumbered and left for dead. I guess the people up north aren't so friendly."

"I guess not." I felt like it was my fault, but maybe it was an association thing. "You didn't have anyone you could call?"

"I'm trying not to get other people involved."

Oh, that just made me incredibly nervous. "This is some kind of legal matter, isn't it?"

"I'm not a criminal," he laughed. "I'm not in a cult. I'm probably much more normal than you."

"No way! I am not a traditionally normal teen, but I am more normal than you. I'm on my way to college to be a doctor."

"Really?" He got an even bigger laugh out of that. "How is college gonna work out when you've barely interacted with anyone your entire life?"

I did a double-take. "How would you know that?"

"You stare at me like you've never seen a boy before. I bet you only let me in your car because you're desperate for human interaction." He had such a smug smirk, and it didn't help that he was very attractive.

"Well, maybe I'm staring because I like looking at your face!" Oh, my gosh! I so did not mean to say that. "I meant I find your face intriguing…or…" I could not stop saying the right things—in the wrong way—at the wrong time. I didn't know what was wrong with me, but he was doing his best to ignore my girlish reactions.

"Look, it's cool you've got this 'I'm a homeschool girl desperately reaching out to be independent' thing going on, but I worry it's gonna get you killed."

"Well, you're not gonna kill me."

He paused, but I think he was just trying to freak me out. "No, I'm certainly not."

"Then, protect me from those who may."

He shrugged and turned to the window. "I suppose I am indebted to you."

We didn't talk for a while. He was very distant and secretive. I would have talked about me, but I didn't want him to really be crazy and end up killing my entire family or something. I couldn't sit in silence. "Why'd you move from Austin?"

"Divorce. My mom fought for custody over me, and I ended up stuck on a farm with her and my grandparents. I would have preferred to stay with my dad, but she needed me more. I don't think she could stand being alone. That's why they divorced. He was always working, and he had a dangerous job."

"Oil rig?"

"He did work on a rig, yes." He smiled, but his voice got quiet and sad. "He died two years ago. Cancer."

I was such a jerk for prying, and now I felt awkward. People around me experienced such awful pain of loss, but I never did. "I'm sorry."

"Don't be. I could be lying to you compulsively. Maybe nothing I say is true." He had a little smirk on his face, so I didn't know if he were or weren't sincerely lying, joking, or really trying to get inside my head.

"We're bound by social media. I can find out if what you say is true in minutes."

He shook his head and looked to the window. "I hate this world we live in."

"It's definitely weird. I wonder what life would be like, sometimes, if someone set off an EMP blast, and we were forced to all go back to the beginning. We'd have to be one with nature. Instead of planning to go shopping for shoes in our downtime, we'd be hunting. Maybe it would be cool to visit those animal instincts of ours again. We're so evolved that we're kind of helpless."

"Like you?"

"Hey, I would have been fine if my 4G was working. The internet would have taught me everything I needed to know." I was part of the problem, but moving away was the first step in the right direction. On top of kissing a boy and cooking my own dinner, maybe I'd learn how to fish or shoot a gun. Maybe I'd become like a super-secret spy or something cool.

The phone rang through the main speaker of the car, and I became worried. I wanted to ignore it, but I think my parents would have quickly called the police. "Is that your parents?"

"Yeah. I should answer them. Don't say anything."

"My lips are sealed." He did seem a little bored, so maybe he would keep his mouth shut.

I pressed the green phone button on my touchscreen. "Hi, Daddy!"

"Hi, sweetheart. It looks like you're not quite on schedule."

"Did you figure out how to track me with GPS?"

"Not with your phone, but the car has a tracker."

"Oh." On top of being embarrassed that he was observing me like an amoeba under a microscope, I was nervous like he actually had cameras in the car. "Well, I had a flat tire."

"Why didn't you call for help?" He kept his voice down, but he was angry.

"Because I'm an adult, and I had enough sense to call for assistance instead of bothering you about it. You can't hold my hand forever. You have to let go eventually."

"It's just hard to."

"I know." I had never lied to my dad before. I wasn't technically lying, but I was going to spill the beans if we kept talking. "I love you. Bye."

"You don't wanna talk a little longer? It must be lonely in that car."

"I'm fine, Dad. I wanna concentrate on the road."

He paused, and I was convinced his dad senses were gonna kick in and alert him to my misbehavior. I was wincing. "Alright. I love you."

"Love you, too." I pressed the red button to end the call and sighed in relief.

"Girls like you are the reason why bad guys win all the time," Maxwell scolded. "I don't understand why you wouldn't tell him about me."

"I don't wanna hear him yell for the next century or have you arrested for attempted rape suspicion."

He stared at me with his mouth hanging low in amazement. "You are a grim little girl."

"Woman." Just because I was a teenager, and he wasn't, didn't mean he got to treat me like a child. I was the one holding the wheel. I had control.

We were very quiet for the next twenty miles or so. We started to see more civilization. I was constantly thinking about my spare tire. I had this fear that it would just pop off and explode. Plus, I had a gnawing hunger. Eventually, I heard a belly rumble, but it wasn't mine.

"Do we need to stop?"

"I'm fine." He turned completely away from me. "I'll deal."

He was so stubborn. I did not imagine that growl. It was like an angry little dog was giving me a piece of their mind. "Well, I'm getting hungry, and I think we need to get that tire anyway. I'm pulling over."

He sighed, but it was a necessary evil. There was a place close to the exit that had a ton of tires in the window. It was shiny, bright, and clean. I didn't think it was some off-brand place. "Do you think this is a fine enough place to get my tire fixed?"

"Sure…" He seemed so disinterested.

I had the employees look at the car. It took them about five minutes to get me to a register while Maxwell sat on a chair looking at the television. "How much is it?"

"You're looking at two-fifty."

"As in 'hundred' dollars?" I didn't mean to raise my voice and sound pathetic or poor, but I was just surprised.

"Of course."

I had plenty of money to live off, but I had a very strict budgeting plan from week to week. I had emergency money, but I didn't know if another emergency would pop up. "I guess I will charge if I can."

"We have a credit card you can apply for."

"Or we can go down the road to one of your colorful competitors and get a slightly used tire for eighty dollars." Maxwell came swaggering with a smirk and stood beside me. "Otherwise, I'm sure you could work something out."

I looked to Maxwell, and he gave me a little nod. I felt confident and stood a little higher with a smirk. "What he said."

The sales associate wasn't too happy, but what could he do? "I'll see what I have in back."

"Thank you!" I was trying to be polite, but I was thankful to Maxwell.

"My former best friend's father was a mechanic. You've gotta be careful and know your market, or else, you're gonna get screwed."

I tried to pat him on the shoulder as a form of camaraderie, but he pulled away very quickly. It was kind of alarming, weird, and hurtful. He noticed. He moved on purpose, but I kept my feelings to myself.

The sales associate came back. "That'll be eighty dollars plus the labor—"

"I'll put it on for her." Maxwell smiled hard at the sales associate struggling not to kill him. In a few minutes, Maxwell was carrying my slightly used tire out to my car.

"I really appreciate you volunteering to change my tire again, Maxwell. Can I just call you Max?"

"No."

"Oh. Okay…" He was a complicated one. I thought we were bonding, but maybe he was just using me for a ride, and I shouldn't have thought there was more to it.

"You should get a new jack. I can't get it to work anymore."

"Oh, so it was freak luck, huh?" I knew I wasn't crazy or that idiotic.

"I guess so."

There was a truck stop joined with a couple of fast-food spots. I was sure I could find what I needed inside. "Fine, but you've gotta let me buy you food."

"I'd rather get back on the road." I wasn't sure, but I think he was annoyed with me.

"What's the rush? There will still be cows in Kansas when you get back home."

He started looking around. His eyes rested on a bus stop, but it was busless. I was his only option. "Fine."

I drove the car over to the truck stop. It seemed kind of rude to change the tire on the tire shop's property, considering Maxwell showed them up so well. I went shopping for my jack and grabbed a couple of energy drinks for the journey. Then, I bought us some food and insisted we eat in a booth. I scooted all the way down, but Maxwell opted to sit across from me instead. I tried not to take it personally. People needed their space.

Maxwell tore into the burger. It reminded me of this dog my parents had when I was little. He was a savage when he ate and very territorial. He was sweet in the house, but he would kill anything that came into the backyard, especially other dogs. He frightened me, so my parents never got another dog when he died. "When was the last time you ate anything?"

I had only eaten a couple of chipmunk bites of my salad, and his burger was already gone. "A day, I guess."

"Well, let me buy you another burger."

"No."

"Aw. Am I upsetting your grown-up man feelings? You need a little girl to buy you something?" It was very exciting, feeling like the older person.

"This is your parents' money, right?"

"Some of it. My grandma gave me a pretty hefty amount as well. They owned an apple orchard."

"So, you're a bit of a farm girl?" He had a little smirk on his face like he liked that about me. Maybe he was attracted to that.

"Kind of…not really. I watched her make cider one time, but that was the extent of it. I didn't spend a ton of time at the orchard."

He intently watched me as I ate. My parents taught me to eat slowly and enjoy my meal. It was better for my digestion. Only a couple of minutes had gone by, but Maxwell was shaking like he had cabin fever. "Maybe I should take a bus or a train. I am kind of in a hurry."

If he took the bus, my parents wouldn't ever have to find out about the colossally idiotic thing I did, but I got a dreadful feeling in the pit of my stomach when he mentioned it. "I'm sort of enjoying my time with you. You've proven to be useful, and I am kind of lonely in the car…" I felt like a loser for even admitting that. I barely knew him.

"How do you feel about me driving when you get tired?"

"So, I can wake up with my spleen missing?" I laughed. "No, thank you!"

He glared at me in a very intimidating way. "Seriously?"

"I'm not that stupid." Could he possibly overcome me and take the wheel? Yes. Was he going to? Maybe, but I wasn't going to invite him to kill me. "I'm gonna try to make it to Missouri, and then, I'm gonna pass out on a comfy bed. You're welcome to join me."

He cocked his brow. "In the bed…?"

"No! No. Absolutely not. You can join me in the hotel—not in my room—in a separate room or…" I was so flustered; I could feel my face melting from embarrassment. "I mean, you're welcome to join me in the car. I don't know what you're gonna do afterward. I'll get you to Missouri faster than a bus. Kansas is right next door."

God bless him for not reacting to my weirdness. If he were as weird as me, I think our awkwardness might have made the entire universe collapse on itself. "Alright. We'll part our ways then."

"Okay." I bought him another burger without his permission, and he did eat it. By the time he finished it, I was done and ready to go. I researched his life while he was changing the tire. He had pictures of lots of friends, but he didn't seem very close to anyone. I mean, he was always smiling like he was happy, but even in party pictures, he was off to the side. I didn't see any posts about girlfriends. That was sort of strange for a guy his age and as hot as him. I never had a boyfriend before, but I had overbearing parents, and I was incredibly antisocial. He seemed to travel a lot. He had friends. I saw a couple of sports pictures, and he was in band and choir. All the stuff he told me about himself proved to be true, though.

I turned on the radio when we got in the car. The silence really bothered me, because I didn't wanna think about what he might have been thinking about—me and my obvious crush on him. The music didn't help when some sexually suggestive lyrics about stalking a crush came on. "What's this crap you listen to?"

"It's pop."

"It's not even good pop."

"And what's 'good' pop?" I don't know why I was getting defensive. I didn't like that stuff either.

"Nothing, but this is just the worst. You have satellite. Why don't we listen to something good?"

"Something country?" I mocked. I could imagine him and his buddy from the pictures tipping cows over to some hoedown garbage. "Something trashy?"

"Or how about classic?" He fiddled around with my radio until it landed on a station playing nothing but music from the forties. I thought he was kidding, but he had the biggest smile on his face and snapped his fingers along with the cool rhythm. "Awesome, right?"

"Yeah." I didn't mean to stalk his face again, but I was baffled. He was extremely rugged, but handsome. He was strong, yet sensitive. He was social, but not a pig. "You don't seem human."

"W-what do you mean?" It was even cute how he stuttered.

"You're just not what I imagine a human male to be like." My parents overreacted about everything, but they made me scared when it came to members of the opposite sex, like if I tripped on him, I'd end up pregnant or something.

"Are you some kind of feminazi or something?"

"No, I just had expectations, and you crushed them. You're fictional."

"I'm…not…?" he chuckled.

"I mean, you're not normal. You're a fantasy guy." I didn't know if it was okay to say all of that. My crush became more obvious by the second, but I didn't mind that he knew. I barely knew him, but what I did know was that he made me feel safe and…uncomfortable, but in a good way.

"When I was in high school, I joined a crooner club because we were cooler than a glee club. We were much more suave. I've always been creative. My former friend and I liked to charm the country gals."

"Oh. It's always about the chicks, right?" Wasn't it utterly ridiculous that I was jealous? "I guess you're more normal than I thought."

"I always had a more sophisticated taste. Most girls in my high school thought sophistication was clogging as your talent in a beauty competition."

We both laughed. I kind of hated my laugh. It made me sound like such a little kid. I didn't want him to think of me as a child. I wanted him to think I was a sophisticated young woman. "That's funny."

"I never really pursued anyone until college, but it never worked out."

"You went to school in Chicago, right?"

"Yeah…" What was I thinking? I made him uncomfortable with my spying again.

"We should have gotten a stuffed pizza when we passed it. I don't know what I was thinking."

"Then you have to go to the right place to get stuffed pizza. They're not all created equal. I've got a great recipe. Maybe I could text it to you when I get a new phone."

"I'd like that." I blushed like we were five in a classroom, and he let me borrow his favorite box of crayons. It was innocent and fresh, and something I had never really felt before. It was so weird— but in a good way.

I kept it on the forties radio station. He sang out a couple of lyrics every so often. He really did have a smooth texture that lulled me further into a sense of security. If he were a serial killer, he certainly was taking his sweet time with me, and I would continue enjoying every moment of my supposed demise.

He got uncomfortable, eventually, and faced the window. He kept his eyes closed as well. "Do you think I could roll down my window? I don't feel very well."

"Do we need to stop?"

"No, I'm okay."

It was loud with the fast wind rushing past our window, but I wanted to be as accommodating as possible. I did catch the grumbling of his stomach again. He grunted and seemed to be in pain. "Are you okay?"

I reached out to touch his arm, but he violently shook away as soon as I grazed him. "Don't touch me!"

I pulled away, extremely startled. It was almost beastly how he spoke. "I'm sorry." I didn't know if he was passing a kidney stone or if he was just genuinely strange, but I didn't feel as safe anymore. "Do you need to go to a hospital?"

"I'm fine. Keep driving."

With all the awkward waiting, my bladder started to get jumpy, and I couldn't really hold myself together. "I've gotta pee."

"Again?" he shrieked.

I did go like twice while we stopped. "I guess I shouldn't have had so much pop. It goes right through me. My parents didn't usually buy it and…" It occurred to me that he wouldn't care what I had to say, and I didn't have to explain myself. He was my disgruntled passenger.

I exploded out of the car so fast to the bathroom that I forgot to grab my purse, and the keys were inside it. I had one of those automatic start cars, so it never left my bag. It didn't occur to me until I relieved myself, but then I had another ton of pressure on me. I washed my hands as quickly as possible and ran for the car. By the time I got out, he was throwing the keys at me.

"You really waste a lot of time." At least he wasn't a thief. If he wanted my money or my car, that was the perfect opportunity. His opinion of my adulthood probably plummeted.

"I'm sorry. I'm just not anxious to be stuck in the car."

"Well—"

There was a growl and a black image in the corner of my eye. I turned and saw a mangy and mean stray coming our way. I was terrified of all dogs, which I blamed on my old dog, so a loose one in the wild really frightened me. I instinctively grabbed my new protector and eye candy for support, but he was even more freaked out when I screamed and grabbed him, and he—quite literally—pushed me to the ground. I landed on the sidewalk and scraped my hand, but I was so caught between being appalled, furious, and still afraid, that it didn't hurt so bad. I closed my eyes and waited for the worst.

"Get out of here!" Maxwell wasn't afraid of the dog. I opened one of my eyes to peek at the danger, and he stepped forward to establish his dominance. He was very intense and growling again. The dog backed away and then just ran.

He looked down at me, and the intensity faded. The color drained from his face, and he was struggling to catch his breath. "I'm sorry, Jesse."

"It's fine." I reached out my hand, but he just stared at it with glistening eyes like he was me and I was the dog. "Are you not going to be a gentleman and help me up?"

He might have been ashamed to do it, but he stuffed his hands into his pockets. "I sort of have this thing about touching people."

My dad had a friend who had a thing with germs, but he wasn't rude. "Okay." I helped myself up, and the whole daydream about meeting a perfect stranger, who was truly my soulmate, began to fade away. He had a quirk. He probably had about ten quirks, and they weren't very attractive.

But for some reason, I was still very attracted to him.

"Why don't you take care of that and stretch your legs?"

I looked at my hands. They were bleeding, and they stung. "Do you not like germs and blood?" I tried to show him my hands as a test, and he walked around to the other side of the car. "Seriously?"

"It's something like that." He took a deep breath again, but he wasn't steadily holding anything in. "I'm gonna get some air. I'll be back in a little while." He literally ran off behind the gas station and to only God knows where. We were still out in the boonies. I didn't think there was anywhere he could run off to, and there was a loose dog somewhere.

I went back inside the gas station to wash and bandage up my hands. There was a pinball machine. I did well in the arcade at a neighbor's birthday party, so I figured I could find a way to pass the time. I died immediately, but I had several quarters on me. I got the hang of it eventually, but time was passing by. I was worried once Maxwell had been missing for fifteen minutes.

I glanced around outside, but I was still kind of scared of the dog, so I got back in my car. Another ten minutes went by before I saw him running through the dark and back inside the gas station like he was avoiding the entire world.

I was worried, so I ran in after him. He headed to the unisex bathroom and locked the door. "Maxwell?" I knocked a couple of times. "Are you okay?"

"I need a minute."

I was really freaking out now. Either something was medically wrong with him, or he was a complete weirdo. Either way, I should have run away screaming. For whatever reason, I didn't. I was concerned more for him than for myself, and I wanted to make sure he was okay. "Maxwell, are you sure you're alright?"

He opened the door a couple of minutes later. "Are you ready to go?"

"Are you kidding me? I've been waiting for you the whole time."

"Oh." He awkwardly put his hands in his pockets and nodded. "Sorry for the confusion. Let's go."

He tried to shuffle away from me, but he clearly wouldn't move past me if it meant I would touch him. I moved out of the way so he could get by. I had been in that bathroom, so I knew if he hated germs, then he wouldn't have been in that crap-infested hole. It was totally unsanitary.

We walked to the car together, but I hesitated to unlock it. He looked at me, but I was having this dilemma.

"Is there a problem?"

"No. I'm just curious about you and where you've been."

"I can try to find another ride if I'm making you uncomfortable." It was frustrating that he was going to choose to be that stubborn.

"Your secrecy is making me uncomfortable!"

"You know a lot more about me than I know about you."

"There's nothing to know about me."

"Really?" He laughed and leaned over the hood suspiciously. "Because there's something very peculiar about you!"

I probably made a blobfish face because I was puzzled, and I felt how disgustingly unattractive my expression was. I made myself a little queasy. "I don't understand what you could mean."

"Fine. Don't explain. I'll trust you, and you'll have to trust me. Either we do, or I walk."

I was dumbfounded. I just didn't get it, but I really didn't want him to leave. When I thought about being alone, I felt panic inside of me. I knew I would think about him. I knew I would miss him. It was stupid, but I was so sure of it. "Let's go."

"Even though I may be a serial killer?" he mocked.

I got so angry with him. "Well, maybe I'm a serial killer! What kind of girl invites a guy into her car? Maybe I'm driving you to Kansas so I can take everybody out. Your mom. Your grandparents. All the little animals, too! Have you ever thought of that?"

"No, but thanks for the visual, I guess…"

I didn't notice a family was getting out of a van, and they might have heard me confess to attempted murder. I just kind of wanted to die after that, so I slipped into the car and pressed my head against the wheel. The horn honked, but I didn't care.

"You're fictional too," Maxwell said as he slipped in after me. "I don't know what to make of a girl like you."

I didn't know why a hunky guy like him was into me. I mean, I think he was into me. I wasn't exactly sure. He must have been! I just threatened his entire family, and he filed that under *quirky* instead of *crazy*. "I'm just a normal girl."

"We'll see."

I ignored him. There was nothing strange coming from me. That was all him! Well, that's what I thought, anyway.

Chapter Three

"I'm an only child." I finally blurted something after an hour of intense silence.

"Excuse me?"

"You wanted to know more about me. I'm an only child. My brother died, so my parents sheltered me. I'm not used to being around other people."

He grinned with an adorable amusement. "I already gathered that, but thank you for opening up."

I racked my brain while trying to think of something remotely interesting to tell him, but my life seemed so vastly boring. "I can play the flute. My parents thought it was important for me to learn how to play an instrument, and the flute was serene and pretty. It was something that wouldn't bother them while I was practicing."

"I can play guitar, drums, and piano."

"You're your own band?" I tried not to be jealous, but I was very impressed. "That's amazing."

"It's too bad I can't split myself up into three people. Besides, my singing voice doesn't honestly go with anything contemporary."

"So? You could reinvent music. You could be something else entirely." Being an only child blessed me with an overactive imagination. I could already see him on a huge stage playing under a flood of colorful lights. "I'm excited for you."

"I don't want to be a music star. It would be too difficult. I just wanted to be more social, so I pushed myself to work with my hands a lot. I took shop. I worked on my grandparents' farm. I cook too."

"Wow." I was crushing even harder than before. "I've never cooked a meal by myself."

"Never?" He was amazed, and it may have been in a bad way.

"Not since I nearly burned down the house when I tried to surprise my parents with breakfast."

"Wow." At least he laughed. "You are quite a force."

"I try." He had such a nice smile. I hoped he didn't plan on growing his beard out further. I wouldn't want him to lose any more of his handsome face. It was gonna suck when I couldn't stare at him anymore.

"Eyes on the road," he warned. "Are you trying to get us killed?"

"I'm paying attention." I was trying not to fall under his spell too much. I knew he was holding back something crucial from me. He might not have been a psychotic killer, but I had a bad feeling he was dangerous.

We had casual talk from here and there, but we mostly listened to the music he liked. It was lovely and all, but I was starting to get tired. I chugged down some energy drinks, but I didn't feel anything for longer than a couple of minutes. I didn't want to fight with myself and wake up dead or worse.

"It's kind of getting late. I'm tired and hungry again."

"We're barely at the tip of Missouri." He could really whine like a baby when he wanted to.

"Okay, but I told you we'd make it. We did. I've got a long drive tomorrow. I need to rest. I promised my parents I would be careful about pushing myself."

He fumed up his face, but what could he say? I had the wheel, and he sure wasn't driving me to my grave. "Fine."

I found a commercial hotel to stop in to avoid ending up at something haunted or something too good for the roaches to dwell in. Maxwell didn't offer an opinion. He was still quietly fuming, even when we parked. "So, we are here."

"We are."

"I can pay for a room for you."

"No. I'd rather not have you do that. You've done enough for me." When he looked at me, I remembered his eyes really popping out, and I was sort of amazed at his raw beauty. "I'm gonna try to find another person to drive me. If I can make it home tonight, I think that would be best."

"Oh." I was bummed, for sure. I didn't like him throwing an ultimatum at me, but we both knew that's what he was doing. "Fine. If you need to get home, you go. I get it."

He wasn't bluffing. He actually got out of the car. I reluctantly got out. I needed to go to my room, and I wanted to say goodbye. I walked around the car and almost wrapped my arms around him, but he took a step back. "Right. You don't wanna touch me…"

He grinned hard and awkwardly.

"Well, goodnight."

"Goodnight."

I grabbed a bag from the back of my car. I had a separate duffel bag for my hotel stays, so I wouldn't have to lug heavy and separate suitcases for a couple of things. I could have asked Maxwell to help me, but I really didn't need him to. It was best to get a clean break. The lingering thing wasn't gonna be good for either of us.

"I'm gonna order a pizza when I get inside. You must be hungry again."

He shrugged. "I could always eat."

"I'll order it, and you can wait in my room."

He blinked a few times, surprised. Then, I felt a chill sweep over us. "That wouldn't be appropriate."

"Oh!" My face was a ball of fire, and I couldn't stop giggling like a silly girl. "I didn't mean anything by it. I was just inviting you in to eat with me. I'll order and bring it to that balcony sitting area. I'm sure that'll be fine."

"Yeah…" I thought Maxwell would be a whole lot cooler than he was. Maybe I was so good at being pathetic that it rubbed off on him. His face looked just as goofy as mine.

I carried my own bag up to my room and collapsed on the bed. I couldn't believe the day I had. Would I be able to even keep such a secret from my parents? I would want to tell someone about Maxwell, one day. I wasn't going to easily forget someone like him. He was gonna be hard to shake like an infection. Maybe he'd always stay with me. Maybe I'd always be changed in whatever way I felt myself changing.

"What is wrong with me?" I had gone through puberty with literally no boys. I missed out on the experience of really liking someone. There weren't any butterflies that made me explode if I didn't get to kiss a boy's lips, or at least tell him how I felt. This was all so new and pungent. I could feel my heart rapidly beating in my chest, my face was flushed, and my skin was all tingly. I didn't know how to make it stop. It was horrible, but it was oddly thrilling.

I ordered the pizza and called my parents. They wanted to make sure they knew exactly where I was. They would have talked with me on the phone forever, but they didn't do anything all day but worry about me, and I didn't want to lie to them. I cut them off as soon as I could.

I changed into a tank top and some comfy pajama pants. After being cooped up in a car all day, I wanted to relax. But when I looked in the mirror, I was a little too relaxed. If I had known I was going to bump into a hot boy, maybe I would have put a little blush on before I left the house. It was stupid, but I put a little something on my cheeks. I didn't want him to mistake me for a zombie.

When the pizza and two bottles of pop came, I walked them over to Maxwell. He was resting his eyes or meditating. I dropped the box on the table and jumped on the couch next to him. "Pizza! Yay."

Maxwell opened his eyes and smiled. "Those are cute pajamas."

"Thank you." I tried to hide my face.

"Were you wearing makeup before?"

"What?"

"Were you wearing makeup before? I didn't notice."

Oh, I was so embarrassed! He probably thought I put it on because it was like we were on a secret date he didn't know about, but now, maybe he had a reason to suspect we were dating! "Maybe you weren't looking hard enough."

I grabbed a slice of pizza and stuffed my face. I couldn't blush and eat at the same time. "This is good pizza!"

"I wish there was meat."

"I'm a vegetarian."

He was so offended; I think he was going to kill me. He literally dropped a slice back in the box from shock.

"It has nothing to do with animal cruelty. I just don't like the texture of meat. I don't care if you eat cheeseburgers and steaks."

"No wonder you're so thin."

I never thought of myself in any other way than just being me. I looked at my arms, and then my boobs. I knew they weren't big, but they were nice in my bra. "Am I too thin?"

"You could probably stand to have a little bit more meat, but you've got a pretty nice body." Maxwell was so casual that I couldn't tell whether he was flirting. He continued scarfing down my pizza until it was gone. I was lucky I got my two slices in.

"You never told me what you were looking for."

"I'm sure you looked at my college major when you were digging. I was researching for a story."

"What kind of story?" He was an animator, for goodness sake. Talking racecars and dancing penguins weren't exactly poetry. "You couldn't have looked it up online?"

"No." I could sense him hesitating again, but he must have known he had a captive audience. I wasn't going anywhere. "I was researching some things about the supernatural. There were some interesting stories about wolves in the U.P., so I came out here to find out the legends and get inspired."

Werewolves were sort of a grim topic for a cartoon. I wasn't really a fan of violence. "What kind of legends?"

"About a pack living up that way. There are stories about packs in Canada, but I figured I should go home after the jumping incident."

"And why did you get jumped?"

"They wanted my money." He drowned his shady story in a bottle of pop. By the time he guzzled what was left, I decided to let it go. He would tell me the truth, eventually, or maybe he would hold off until it didn't matter. He was, supposedly, about to jump on the back of a truck and be permanently out of my life forever.

"I wanna be a doctor," I said. "I think it's important to make an impact on the world. I don't wanna fade away and have no one know I was ever here to begin with."

"Simple lives are important too. Creating a family with respectful children would be monumental. If you could keep them safe and happy, mad props to you." It was sweet that he cared so much. His eyes sort of sparkled, so maybe he thought seriously about starting his own family. I knew he'd be a good dad. I could sense it.

"I think I'd like to be a hero." Superpowers were great, but healing a sick child would have meant more to me than flying or having super strength.

Maxwell sank into his chair like he was about to throw his head back and go to sleep. "You're sweet."

I enjoyed the compliment, but I also didn't. I wasn't a child. I did look young, but I also looked like a woman. "I'm more than sweet, though. I've got some bite to me."

"I don't doubt it." He smirked a little bit, and he gave a look that was telling me it was okay to go in for the kill, but he wasn't moving. I was confused. Wasn't a boy supposed to be the one to initiate the whole lip-lock thing?

"Thank you for dinner." He stood up and grabbed his backpack. "I'm gonna go try to get a ride."

Did I have pizza crust stuck in my teeth? Did I suddenly grow a third eye? "Yeah. You go do that." I stood up to at least hug him, but he took a step back again. He must have had a legitimate tick, but it was getting sort of hurtful. "Good luck."

"Thank you." He grabbed his backpack and seemed to lean in for a hug, but he definitely moved away, and I made an idiot out of myself when I tried to hug him again. "Well, it's been fun."

"Bye." I waved like a lame loser. I stood alone for a little while, hoping he would turn around and come back to me, but he didn't. I watched him from the balcony to make sure he wouldn't run back to me in a romantic gesture and kiss my pathetic lips.

I went back to my room and collapsed on my bed. I barely knew him. It shouldn't have mattered that he was gone. I didn't understand how he could be under my skin so much. I think it was worse that he didn't kiss me. Now, instead of missing the touch of his lips, I was always gonna wonder what they felt like. I would always wonder if the curiosity was worth it, and it killed me that I would never know.

I was tired, yet I couldn't sleep for the longest time. When I finally crashed, I slept well through my alarm. It was already past ten-thirty, but I took a chance and ran down to the dining area to see if the free breakfast was already gone. They were taking back the last of the juice as I came in.

I pouted and hung my head in defeat. I almost missed Maxwell sitting in the lobby, reading the paper on a chair. "What are you doing here?"

"I couldn't get anyone else blinded by such radiant kindness to take in a poor mutt like me, so here I am." He smiled like all was supposed to be forgiven, and he didn't just ditch me.

I crossed my arms to play hard to get. "You stayed outside the entire night?"

"I did, but I'm okay. I found a nice tree to sleep under, for a couple of hours, before the police asked me to leave." He stood up and walked close to me. It was the closest he had been yet, and he was still really cute, even though he had on the same clothes as yesterday.

"Well, you sort of smell. I'm gonna let you use my bathroom to wash up. Then, we can go on our merry way." I tried to retain my false anger. He did abandon me, after all. He should have been super gracious that I allowed him to come into my hotel room.

"I really appreciate you doing all of this for a stranger. I won't forget this."

"Well, you scratched my back first. I'm returning the kindness."

Maxwell took off his jacket and hung it up neatly. Then he pulled off his hoodie, and it pulled his shirt up, so I got a glance at his beautifully sculpted abs. I bashfully smiled and even giggled. I had seen an underwear commercial or two, so I knew what a man's body looked like, but I hadn't seen one up close and personal before. Maxwell was oblivious or, at least, pretending to be. He took off his socks and shoes and went inside the bathroom with his backpack.

I dressed while I heard him in the shower. I had on a pair of shorts, a tank, and a plaid shirt that I kept unbuttoned. I had my dark brown hair in a messy braid before. I didn't know if I should wear it up or down, but I decided to go for it again. I did put makeup on this time—a little blush, mascara, and gloss—so I would look a little more appealing.

I was all packed and ready to go by the time he came out of the bathroom, smelling fresh, and in a tighter pair of jeans and a T-shirt. I put the dirty hoodie in a laundry bag, so if he didn't wear his jacket, he was going to be showing me his arms all day. "You're pretty cut. Did the guitar give you those guns?"

"No. I did cross-country running. I lifted weights. I swam. I've got a punching bag in the barn."

"I would have pegged you for football."

"I always wanted to play." He smiled, but there was a flash of regret in his eyes. "I think I would have been great, but I have this thing about contact. I'm not used to letting people so close to me physically…"

Contact. Physical. Those were the words that ruled my thoughts when he spoke, and I was standing close to him already. He must have trusted me. He changed his mind about my hotel room being inappropriate. Was he crushing on me the way I was crushing on him? I didn't know, but I certainly needed to.

I had no idea what I was doing, but I grabbed his face and crashed my lips right into his. I had never touched someone else's lips before, but I was sure he was supposed to be moving his mouth, so we could make out. He actually wasn't moving at all.

I opened my eyes and noticed his horrified expression. By horrified, I mean his eyes were bulging out of his sockets, and the color drained from his face again. He was even shaking. I drew away in great concern for what was happening to him. Maxwell's feet and hands were frozen. "What was that?"

"I'm sorry!" If that were a normal bed, I would have crawled underneath it while I died. "I thought that was the moment to do something like that. Was I wrong?"

Maxwell's feet became unstuck, but he was stumbling around like the entire room was spinning. He broke out into a sweat as if my lips were made of habaneros. He kept wiping his cheeks and lips like he'd rather rub his skin off than have my lingering touch be a part of him.

"Maxwell?"

Finally, it became too much for him, and his nausea rose to a level that couldn't be contained. He ran inside the bathroom, and I heard him vomiting. I kissed a boy for the very first time in my life, and he ended up vomiting. It wasn't even casual vomiting. It was gut-wrenching vomiting like someone was punching him in the stomach and choking him to death.

"I'm sorry…" I was so embarrassed that I ran from the room and down the stairs. I made a complete fool out of myself, and my nightmare would probably never ever end.

Awesome.

Chapter Four

I ended up sitting outside the hotel. There was a stone bench where I could sulk alone in my utter disgust. I never wanted my first kiss to be anything like that, and yet, I wasn't surprised it could happen to me. I was just a freakshow.

Maxwell came out of the hotel with our things, put them down on the ground, and then sat next to me with his back facing the opposite direction from mine. Maybe he was too disgusted to face me. "Was it that bad?"

"No. It wasn't you." I looked at him, and he was deeply mortified about something. "I've never had a girlfriend because I suffer from haphephobia."

I really hoped that didn't mean he got the urge to spontaneously kill people. "What does that mean?"

He mumbled it out so quietly, I'm surprised I even heard his confession. "It means I'm afraid of touch."

"That's really a thing?" I didn't mean to be rude, but it was outrageously strange. "You're not messing with me?"

"I wish I were." He laughed at himself sadly. "I couldn't even hug my mother at my father's funeral without turning into a basket case. I've been trying to get over it for years, but I can't quite get a handle on it."

He was emotionally going through something, but it was sort of a huge relief that there was someone as lame as me in the world. "Were you born with this, or did something trigger it?"

"You must not have dug deep enough into my past."

"I didn't get past social media." I didn't think I needed to. What did I need to know other than that every single selfie he took was hot, especially his duck face?

"When I was a child, my sister and I were kidnapped. She was killed, but I ended up escaping."

Something about his story sounded strange, as if it were familiar. "Really?"

"Yeah. I blocked most of it out, but I've never been the same since then. It was mild at first, but it got worse."

When I looked through his pictures, he was never holding or even touching anyone. It made sense, but I didn't understand why he would risk being so social. "How have you had such a normal life?"

"Everyone around me knows. I went to parties. I was active in school. No one messed with me because they didn't know if I'd break down or go feral if they touched me. Rich helped me a lot, too. He was like my brother."

"Why is he your former best friend?"

"Rich crossed some lines he shouldn't have. He's not the same person he used to be." There was a particular glare in his eye. It was that feral part he warned me about, and I didn't want to push him...at least, not right then.

"I'm sorry to hear that."

He took a deep breath and stared at his hands for a while. I couldn't imagine not hugging my parents when we said goodbye or feeling their kisses before bedtime. Smiles and hugs release endorphins to make you feel good. It was chemistry. It must have been so lonely living as he did. What sort of person would be created in a world so dark?

"I know you're starting to like me." He leaned back and looked into my eyes, and I was trapped in his gaze. I knew it would have been terrible to kiss him, but I was honestly dying to try again.

I couldn't even speak without my face smiling hard enough to hurt. "Is it that obvious?"

"I'd appreciate it if you didn't." He was literally freaking nuts. He shouldn't have hurt me the way that he did, but it cut like a dull knife, ripping my heart into shredded pieces.

"I'll try to honor your wishes..." I turned my head and struggled not to cry. I wanted to experience change. I boldly liked a boy. I kissed him. I even got my heart kind of broken. Why was I broken? I didn't know, but my mascara was starting to burn, so I had to pull myself together. "We should get on the road."

Maxwell waited on the hood of my car while I called my parents before checkout. I had to tell them where I was, but the conversation didn't last long. I spent a little extra time alone researching Maxwell's condition. Haphephobia was a real thing. People who suffered from it experienced pain when they touched someone. They also felt extremely invaded. He probably felt like a rape victim when I kissed him. I was such a tool.

I'm surprised he wanted to travel with me at all, but I suppose he didn't have any choice. There was something mentally wrong with me for deciding to drive him, and I was only getting more bonkers by the second. I wanted to respect his wishes and mine, but I had a difficult time shaking the urge to kiss him again. The tingly feeling all over my body wouldn't go away. I hoped there was more at work than my hormones, but I was starting to feel like a slut for continuously staring at his face.

"Boom!" I hit the steering wheel when I saw a statue of a giant chicken. It was quirky like the two of us. It was going to be perfect. "There's breakfast."

"We should keep moving."

"You can't tell me you're not hungry!" I heard his stomach growl twice.

"I'm starving, but—"

"We are not far from Kansas. Come on. Enjoy a meal with me." I tried the puppy eyes and threw in a child pout for good measure. I don't know if it worked because I was awesome, or because he still didn't have a choice. Maxwell huffed and puffed, but he didn't bother to tear my request down.

So, the chicken was a mascot of a six-dollar buffet, and it was delicious. Even though all the meat looked very appealing, and by the piles stacked on Maxwell's plate, I assumed it was as good as it appeared. I stuffed myself on yummy French Toast, with an apple syrup topping, and whipped cream. "Yummy!"

We were both ripping through our plates fast, so I didn't notice how miserable Maxwell was until I was down to my last piece. "How is food not making you happy?"

"I'm sort of on a deadline. I've got to get home as soon as possible."

I fought with the sense of rejection that washed over me. "You'll be there today. Chill out."

He tapped on the table and slouched, but I don't know why. I knew he was going to get another plate stacked with meat, which he did ten seconds later.

"Tell me about Rich. Maybe I can mend your relationship."

He snickered. "You don't know the first thing about relationships."

"I had a best friend once!" I harped very offendedly. "When I was like three—"

"Three?" he laughed. "Did she steal chalk from you?"

He continued to laugh while a cold chill swept across my body. "That's not funny. How did you know I was gonna say that?"

He cocked his brow and calmed down. "Well, my sister, Annie, got into a fight with a neighbor girl once over—"

"Pink chalk?" I remembered the residue on my little fingers. I remembered a little girl's freaky, but ultra-pretty, catlike eyes. She had chubby cheeks and a frilly blue dress for playing in the mud.

He leaned in almost like he was about to touch me in amazement. "Jessica? Is your name Jessica? Sister of Kevin?"

My head got so fuzzy. I never remembered much about the little girl. I recalled screaming about the chalk, and she ran inside the house with it. The memory always ended when I looked down at our unfinished daisy. Suddenly, I could see someone else by her door. There was a little boy.

My hands were trembling, and I had never been so afraid for my life as at that moment. "I never lived in Austin. How do you know these things?"

"Calm down. I'm not gonna hurt you." Well, him not threatening me to stay calm wasn't going to make me stay calm!

The restaurant was packed full of people, and there were a lot of them taking pictures with their cell phones as they goofed off. I didn't think he was going to kill me in front of all of them. He seemed like a conservative psychopath. "I never told anyone about that memory. Nobody knows about that little girl."

"She ran inside the house crying." Maxwell's eyes glistened. "She said you were mean, but I stuck up for you. I went outside to play with her instead, and we were taken that day."

My chest was tight, and I couldn't breathe. I could barely even think. I didn't know my brother. I saw some pictures of Kevin's smiling face, but they were suddenly so real to me. I could see him holding me in the yard. "I'm sorry. I have to leave."

"Jessica!"

I scooted out of the booth and made a run for my car. I thought I was fast enough to leave Maxwell behind, but when I looked behind me to double-check, he was gone. "Jessica, wait!"

I screamed from nearly bumping into him. I was certainly freaked out by how abnormally fast he was, and the fact that he blocked me from my car. "Do not call me that! That's not my name!"

People would always ask if my name was short for Jessica, and it upset me for some reason. When I heard it, my body shivered like the name was whispered on my neck by a stranger intent on hurting me. "How do you know me? Is this some kind of setup? You knew me when I stopped, didn't you? Did you blow out my tire?"

He moved out of the way before I could push him. "I didn't do anything!" He seemed genuinely freaked out. "Are you working for someone?"

I threw my hands out and screamed. "Who would I be working for, Maxwell?"

"Forget I asked."

"No!" I knew his story about researching wolves for a cartoon was bogus. He was dangerous. "I need to know what's going on."

"I'm just trying to get home. Please!" He was desperate and pleading with me sincerely. I wasn't misreading that, but there were lots of secrets weirder than his fear of touching people.

"Please, get away from me. I need some space."

"We need to leave—"

"I need some space!" I flailed my arms rapidly toward his face, and that scared him off enough to keep his distance from me, so I could jump in my car. I locked the door and started it up. He was giving me a really sad and pathetic look, and I was compelled to help him out. I just needed time to think, and I couldn't do it under a giant chicken.

I drove a mile away to an open field. I cried for no reason. Well, I guess I cried because I didn't understand anything about myself. My dead brother's name was Kevin, and there was no way for Maxwell to know that. Even if he lied about having a phone and looked me up on social media, I never mentioned anything about Kevin. I didn't even remember him. My parents never talked about him. It was too painful.

I needed to know if I lived in Austin. I did ask my parents where I was born, and they told me Clearwater General. That's what they said, and they would never lie to me. Never.

But I had to know for sure.

My parents did give me files, like my social security card and birth certificate. I had to unpack my car to get to the right box. Under a photo album—that was literally stuffed with pictures of my parents and me—I found it. I had seen it before, but I don't think I ever read it. My mother got my documents together when I took my driving test. It said I was born in the right hospital in Michigan, but I just couldn't shake my uneasiness.

I looked at a couple of other things from my box of memories. I found a picture of me when I was about four, while with my grandparents. I was crying in the picture as if I were afraid of them, and that always seemed hysterical to me. But now that I looked at it harder, maybe I didn't recognize them. I mean, I didn't look like them, and neither did my dad. Was there a reason why I wasn't close to them?

I looked through more of my pictures. I scanned every photo album with my parents one night, and we saved it all on a flash drive. I plugged it up to a tablet and looked through everything, and I didn't see pictures of me younger than four, besides one baby picture. Wasn't that strange? Considering how much they treasured Kevin, there must have been a picture of me playing with him in the yard, at our house, or my grandparents' orchard.

Then, I swiped to one picture that was probably left in accidentally. I remembered coming across it while I was alone with one of the older albums. I didn't see a lot of pictures with my brother, and it was the only one I saw with a friend. The little boy who Kevin had his arm wrapped around wasn't sporting a manly beard, but it was certainly Maxwell's little face. They both wore cowboy hats and had chocolate stains on their lips and cheeks. They were in the stands at a rodeo.

I sat in my backseat crying over that tablet. It seemed like such a silly lie, yet it felt so monumentally massive. Why would my parents lie about something like where I lived? My birth certificate must have been a forgery. Were all the people in my life a lie? Were they afraid I would want to go back to Austin? Were we in witness protection? I was old enough to know if we were. I needed to know who I was, so I could not tell people!

I didn't have a choice. I had to call my parents. They were probably waiting to hear about my boring road trip.

"How is Missouri, sweetheart?" His soothing voice was suddenly not so charming.

"It's fine, Dad. I stopped at a buffet this morning. It was really good."

"I'm glad. You're not back on the road. It's late in the afternoon. What are you doing?" I also had to wonder if there were other reasons why he always kept me under his thumb. There was this entire story to my life that I had the right to write myself, but it was already written, and the pages were missing.

"I got the urge to look through some of my memories, and I found a picture of Kevin with a childhood friend that seemed really familiar to me." I couldn't involve Maxwell in my quarrel if I wanted Dad to stay on topic. If I told my dad that I picked up a hitchhiker, he would have had me apologizing in tears by the time he got done fussing. "For some reason, it was taken in Austin. Do you know why?"

I winced as I waited in silence for his huge confession. "It's because we used to live there until you were about four."

"Why didn't you tell me?"

"There's nothing to tell—"

"Dad, why are you lying to me?" I was hoping I was misreading him, and everything was a huge coincidence between Maxwell and me, and I was truly being over-the-top paranoid.

"This isn't a conversation I want to have over the phone."

"Then we should have had it in person!" I couldn't believe I snapped at my dad. I wanted to apologize, but I didn't want to lose my nerve. "You need to tell me the truth."

Dad took a long and heavy breath. I could hear every inch of air that exited his mouth, and the weight of his suffering expanded into a massive cloud. "We moved when your brother died. We needed to start fresh."

"And he died from a car accident?"

"No, sweetheart. He was kidnapped." I had never heard my father cry before—that I could remember—but he was getting choked up, and I couldn't stand to hear him in such pain. "By the time the police found the kidnapper's place, he had been killed."

I covered my mouth and sobbed into my hand. I couldn't even remember my brother or the other children taken, and I felt guilty about it. Somehow, I survived unscathed. Why did I deserve to be so fortunate? Would we all have survived if I hadn't supposedly stolen Annie's pink chalk? "Why didn't you tell me this?"

"Because we faced such a trauma, and so did you. You were taken with the other children, and the man who did it was never caught. We always felt like we were being watched, but the police thought we were being paranoid. No one would help us. We were so afraid of losing you again; we packed up everything and started a new life."

Everything was coming full circle, and I didn't understand why. I didn't mean to make that horrible moment about me, considering that Kevin and Annie died, but the sense of betrayal was awful, and it ached. "You should have told me this."

"I'm so sorry, Jesse, but—"

I hung up on my father, for the first time in my life, and I didn't know when I'd want to speak to him again. I lay back in my car and sobbed miserably. It was best I didn't remember, but I wanted to know more. I needed to. The only person I could trust was a stranger, yet I could still sense great danger looming.

Chapter Five

About a half-hour later, Maxwell wandered over. I was still bunched up into a ball and moping on the floor of my car. I had stopped crying. I had nothing left to leak. "Did you learn the truth?"

I nodded and sat up, but my head was throbbing from tears. I turned on the tablet and handed it to him. When he recognized his old friend, I thought he was going to have the saddest and happiest heart attack of all time. "How well did you know my brother?"

"We were pretty close." He sat next to me and unexpectedly smiled. "He was a master at Freeze Tag."

I laughed, but it made me more emotional. I didn't know my brother was old enough, when he died, to have such a good friend. It was sort of like discovering another part of him was still living. "I don't really remember you."

"I vaguely remember you. You wore pigtails like my sister. I think she copied you." He looked at me like he recognized me, and it felt nice—like I shouldn't be so afraid of what I felt. "A lot of my childhood is a blur. The kidnapping was traumatic for me."

"Do you know why we were taken?" I asked.

"No, and I don't know why I survived. You must have gotten out before me. The police found me alone."

I tried to remember seeing him as that little chubby-faced kid. I looked through enough pictures on the web to know him. I just didn't, and I certainly didn't remember being kidnapped. "Don't you think this is strange?"

"It's extremely strange."

What were the odds that we would know each other, move away, and then bump into each other on a road trip? I must have been falling into someone's or something's hands. "Do you believe in Fate?"

"Fate for what?" The clueless look on his face was adorable. He sort of had a crooked grin, and while most people would have seen that as an imperfection, I thought of it as another quirk that set him apart. Though...the quirk about him being afraid to touch me wasn't exactly a good thing. I mean, it was quite horrible, but it's not like I was afraid to touch him. Not that I wanted to touch him! Not inappropriately, anyway...

"Nothing." I shook my head and laughed. I got the tingly feelings all over again. "I'm gonna take you home. Then, I think it's best if we part ways."

"Why?" I was kind of baffled by how confused he was, considering our conversation from earlier.

"I'm trying to start a life, and I can't do it like this. This is very bizarre and distracting!" I hadn't forgotten about wanting to be a doctor, and I couldn't stop. I wouldn't stop.

"Alright. I'll pack your things back up." He hopped on his feet and picked up my boxes and luggage. I wasn't a very perceptive person, but he seemed a little down about something other than kidnapping, murder, and a hazy and violent past.

"Thank you for all of the manly things you do on my behalf."

"Well, thank you for doing the stupid thing and pitying me enough to drive me home."

"Yeah..." I was sure about my decision, but I didn't know if I was content with it. I even liked watching him pick up things and put them down. He took his jacket off, and his muscles flexed like nobody's business. I contained my girlish giggles to myself and got back in the car.

It was getting warmer, so I took off my plaid shirt. I always preferred warmer weather, so it was gonna be nice living in Arizona. I guess it had something to do with me growing up in a warmer climate. Still, it was probably wondrous the first time I saw snow.

After a lot more driving, I noticed some sort of birthmark on his arm. It was dark, like light brown ink, and super intricate. It was like a crescent moon and other neat doodles. "That's a pretty interesting mark."

"It's nothing." I thought it was nothing until he attempted to casually tell me it wasn't.

"You know, after everything that's going on, I hope you know you can trust me."

"It's not that I don't trust you. I just don't want to pull you into my mess of a life. You said you wanted to part ways with me anyway. The fewer questions you ask, the better."

I decided to let it go out loud, but I was still very curious about him. He was a long-lost friend of a brother I didn't quite remember. What would have happened if I hadn't moved away? Would I have grown up with an inappropriate crush on him, hoping that, one day, he would see me for more than a child? Would he still have his touch phobia? Would I have watched him date other girls while jamming out to bad, catchy pop songs about how he should have been with me instead? Then, one day, would he have realized I was all grown up and absolutely perfect for him?

"Remember when you promised not to like me?" he asked.

"I do."

He swallowed the lump in his throat. "I need you to stop trying to seduce me."

"What?" I shrieked. "How am I trying to seduce you?"

"You're biting your lip, and you keep touching them and your chest. You took off your plaid top, so you have more skin exposed. You keep posing in suggestive positions, and you keep staring at me with smirks and side-eyes. It's very obvious."

"I'm not trying to be obvious. I'm not even trying to be subtle." I was mortified and highly impressed with myself at the same time. "I'm not doing anything on purpose!"

"Well, I'd appreciate it if you could make more of a conscious effort."

"Are you kidding me?" I shrieked. "Why did you take off your jacket?"

"Because it's hot—"

"It's because you're hot, and you want me to know it!" And there, I completely screwed up again! "What does this even matter? You can't even touch me."

"I have a mental disorder. I'm not impotent!"

The car quieted down until only the sound of the engine running and the car blazing against the road could be heard. My cheeks were on fire, though. "So…you're attracted to me?"

He stubbornly slouched in his seat. "You say that as if you don't know you're pretty."

I tried to hide my bashful face, but it was hard when I had to keep my eyes on the road. "Maybe I'm not as confident as I should be."

"Well, confidence was never my problem. I've always been sure of myself, and I think I could be great at a lot of things if I weren't such a freak."

I did feel bad for him, but I was also high up on a cloud. He did find me attractive! If I did decide to have anything to do with him, I could work with the "no-touch" thing somehow. "Have you sought professional help?"

"As much as we could afford."

People get over social anxiety all the time. We could work it out…if it mattered. It didn't, though. We were going to part ways forever. We had to.

Another food stop and two bathroom breaks later, we wandered further off the beaten path. There were fields just full of corn and hardly any recognizable signs, but Maxwell seemed to know where we were going. He was like an anxious dog pressed against the window. "We're almost there."

I became miserably sad. "I'll miss you, Maxwell. Do I still have to call you 'Maxwell'? I like calling you 'Max'. Or how about something like 'Maxy'? That's cute, right? Or does it make you think too much of a maxi pad?"

He slowly turned and glared at me in raw confusion and bewilderment. "It wouldn't have, but now you've brought that up, it's completely off the table." He shook his head, but he thought I was funny or pathetic enough to laugh at. "You used to say that when we were little."

"Really?"

"You and Annie…" I felt awful for not being able to miss my brother the way his eyes told me he missed his sister. "I like my full name, please."

Nicknames were a sign of endearment, and we clearly weren't there yet. Maybe we used to be, but that didn't matter anymore. "Okay, Maxwell."

I continued to drive through the extremely remote land. From the road, I could see smoke rising and spreading into an untamable flame. "Is that a fire?"

Maxwell eased up close to the dashboard and breathed very slowly, but harshly. His hands were shaking, but he wasn't getting sickly pale like when I kissed him. He was something else entirely. "No. No. No!"

"I'm gonna call the police." I tried to dial the number on my touchscreen, but he snapped at me.

"No, just drive me to the land!"

"Maxwell—"

He turned to me and yelled right in my face. "Just drive!" He hadn't really frightened me before, but he changed. He growled so aggressively like he wasn't entirely human, and I swore his eyes were brighter than I remembered.

I stepped on the pedal and hoped I stumbled on the wrong address, and Maxwell's family was somewhere safe, and not on the property raging in fire. I prayed there was some sort of mistake, but Maxwell was becoming frantic and angrier.

I parked in front of the house, and Maxwell jumped out and ran into the building without hesitation. I wasn't quite so reckless, but I wished I could have stopped him. "Maxwell!"

It was furiously hot, and I was very intensely afraid of fire. I guess it was just because it was so rapidly uncontrollable, and I wasn't used to being in a state of unexpected behaviors. Having Maxwell in my life was very unpredictable, but I felt safe with him for some reason, and he made me feel alive. When he agreed to protect me, I believed him. I was so afraid for him that my teeth were chattering, and I certainly wasn't breathing. But through the chaos, I just knew he would somehow survive. He was a survivor. That was his constant I could hold onto, even though fire had a constant too.

It burned.

"Maxwell!" I was starting to freak out a lot. I was no tracker, but there were lots of tire marks that looked very fresh. I wasn't sure if it was an accident or not, but someone else was there before we arrived. "Maxwell!"

I heard a crash, and I looked up at a second-story window as glass and wood exploded when Maxwell's body flew through it like a clumsy angel confident in its indestructibility. But he landed on his feet gracefully with a limp and bloody body of a woman in his arms. "Maxwell…?"

The veil of his heroics quickly tore away and revealed a child lost, afraid, and alone. He sobbed miserably over the woman. I thought I was too afraid and queasy to approach them, but my feet walked on their own until I was close enough to see the carnage unleashed on her body. Her throat was ripped apart by some sort of giant claw marks and bitten. There were bite marks all over her, and her flesh was torn apart. The skin on her arm was hanging like a ripped glove. Most notably, her chest had been burrowed through like I was carving into a tub of ice cream to dig out my favorite flavors in Neapolitan. Something purposely went for her chest. I didn't want to look, but I couldn't draw my eyes away from the horrible sight and the effect it was having on Maxwell.

"No!" He gripped her tight and rocked back and forth. I didn't know if his haphephobia was making him shake in pain or if he had suffered far too great a loss to handle, but I knew it wasn't good to hold her like that. "Mama, no…"

"Maxwell…" The house was still notably on fire, and it wasn't coming to an end. "I should call the police."

"No," he seethed. "Don't call them."

"What?" Arson. Murder. It was clear some sort of cult was acting out against him, and they were probably the same people who hurt and left him abandoned in Michigan, and since I was conveniently present, my imagination led me to believe they might have also been the same people who kidnapped us as children. "I have to call the police, Maxwell."

"Leave me alone…" He hid his face, but I could see his entire body racking with what I thought was guilt. He grunted and growled like he was locked in some kind of revenge fantasy and stabbing his attackers to death.

I couldn't wait anymore, because I sure wasn't going to die from smoke ventilation, because the air was too hot when I breathed it in. We were leaving, even if it meant pulling on his clothes to make him move. "Maxwell, we have to go!"

I tried to touch his shoulder and force him to keep moving. However, he sensed me coming, and he turned to scream at me with a face I didn't recognize. "Leave me alone!" His eyes changed into gold, but that was mild compared to the canine-like fangs and claws protruding from the fingers that held his mother's body. He was a monster, and he began to make less sense to me instead of more. But the only sense I could make of anything was the fact that I needed to run.

I rushed to my car, but he leaped above my head and landed in front of the door before I could reach it. He was still growling, and my eyes were drawn to his nasty brown claws. I think that's when I started screaming. No one could blame me for being afraid and running away, but he was too fast and jumped in front of me before I could cross the road. "What are you?"

Maxwell took a deep breath and calmed himself. The nails retracted back inside of his fingers—which seemed super painful to me—and his fangs shrank as well. His eyes were still very much like an animal's. "I think you know what I am, Jesse."

I hesitated to say the word that was too utterly ridiculous to be true, but he was too frightening and strange not to be the fictional creature I already suspected him to be. "A vampire?"

"A vampire?" he shrieked, highly offended. "I have fangs all across my mouth, wolf-like eyes, and claws, and you think I'm a vampire?"

"I meant werewolf!" I yelled in a panic. "I just said vampire because…" I shrugged. I swear I had a broken brain. "I guess every silly teenage girl secretly wants to say that about their crush. I blame young adult novels!"

He rolled his eyes at me. Again, I was an immature child.

But despite seeing the same man I shared a car with, I quivered in my knees and fingers. "I'm really sorry about your mom, but I'm genuinely afraid for my life right now, so I kind of want to go to college immediately."

I knew he wasn't going to touch me, but I still stepped away from him when he tried to approach me. He stopped, a little startled. He was ashamed that he frightened me, and he was still too terrified to grab me. He was probably more likely to kill me than restrain me. I either had to trust him, or I was probably going to die.

"I'm not gonna hurt you, Jesse. I will explain everything to you. I promise. I just…" I was definitely afraid, but the pain shining through his eyes, like a blinding light, was as human as it gets. I didn't think monsters could cry, and if they could, maybe they weren't so bad after all. "I need to do something with my mother's body."

The fire was still spreading. You'd think the police would have arrived with it being so massive, but we were so far out from everything and everyone. Maybe no one would ever come to help poor Maxwell, and maybe no one should have. After all, there was a reason why he didn't want me to call the police.

"You should probably let it burn." I had to look away. I couldn't watch him look at me the way he did. I felt like such a horrible person, and he was just a boy who didn't wanna be alone. "No one would understand this sort of brutality, and you can't afford to tip them off to what you are."

I closed my eyes and winced from the anticipation of his outburst, which was a battle cry of unquenchable fury and immeasurable anguish. It was like an animal nearing the end of life. Whether it was his own or someone else's death prophesied into existence was yet to be discovered.

Maxwell's mother was still lying in that field. His arms fell like wet noodles to his side, and his cautious feet stumbled over the smallest of things. Considering his condition, I knew it must have been difficult for him to pick up his mother. He had to be devastated when he walked her to the front porch and kissed her forehead. He was shaking, and I didn't know if it was only because of his phobia or if it was also because his grief was too much to be contained. But it was extremely difficult to allow him back in my car and watch him grieve without a way to comfort him. I wanted to hug him, like my parents had done to me a thousand times when I was afraid or hurt, but comfort would have been the worst thing in the world to him.

"I need you to drive to Rich's house."

I looked at him twice, and then a third time for good measure. "Rich? Your former best friend who crossed a line? A line that I'm assuming is eating people?"

"I need to find him." His grief was subsiding, and it was being replaced with pure rage. I guess the side effects were his shining eyes and set of fangs. I didn't look at his hands, because the claws really did freak me out. I was concerned about what would happen if his anger continued to expand rapidly while I denied him his outlet.

"Fine! Don't wolf out on me."

"I'm trying not to!" He thrust his head back into the seat and grunted. I couldn't imagine what it must have felt like to transform. Having braces in my mouth sucked enough, so a second set of teeth growing in must have been weird.

I was concerned that a deer or a moose was going to jump in front of my car and break it to pieces, but I kept to the maximum speed, so I could put his mind to rest. Apparently, Rich's house was the next house over, but about five miles down. I freaked out at the thought of an army of werewolves waiting to take us out when we pulled up to his cute little home. It was even painted white and lavender. I didn't believe anyone dastardly could be living in there. All the lights were on, but it was a little too quiet. "This is his place?"

"Stay in the car."

"Really?" I didn't wanna meet Rich, but I didn't wanna bump into him without my super-strong werewolf ally.

"Really."

I wasn't going to argue with him while he was still wolfing out. He was so strong; he accidentally yanked the front door off when he tried to see if it was locked. I was glad he left out in such a hurry that he didn't shut the car door, because he probably would have broken the whole thing.

It sure was unnerving being outside all alone. I crawled over, shut his door, and locked the car like three times. I didn't know if that would help, though. I assumed a werewolf could break the glass and rip my throat out long before Maxwell could return to the car and save me. It was amazing how you could hear all the little things out in the wilderness. I could hear croaking, hooting, and chirping (I guess from crickets). Those things were freaking me out and making me ten kinds of anxious. I was gripping the steering wheel so tightly that I was kind of hurting myself.

Then, I jumped as I heard all sorts of crashes and smashes from within the house. I heard growling, but I was pretty sure those were only the distinctive growls of Maxwell having an angry breakdown. Then, he stopped smashing things and yelled very loudly, which caused a chain reaction of other howls from other things. I didn't think I heard any other werewolves, but I was scared enough to start tearing up.

Maxwell came out of the house de-wolfed, but still furious. "Please, don't slam my door!"

He sort of glared at me. I think he was a little sad he couldn't break my car into pieces, but he did gently close the door. "His parents are dead. His brother and sister are missing."

I had a horrible ache in my chest. I just couldn't believe someone could hurt their own parents, and I wanted to go back home, have my mom hold me, and never ever let go again. "Do you think they got away?"

"The cars were missing, so they could be out somewhere, or Rich and his pack took them."

"His pack?" I was so not equipped to handle a werewolf gang.

"He has a group following him. I can smell them. He's cutting ties to his humanity, and he's forcing me to do the same."

I was a tie, wasn't I? If I got caught with him, I was probably going to be killed. I certainly had more motivation to run away, but I didn't want to always wonder about Maxwell. If I did, I'd get curious and would want to see him again. "So, I gave you some space to grieve. I need some answers now."

He was still reeling on about everything, but he nodded. "The police will probably be out this way soon. We've gotta get out of here."

"And go where?"

"I know a place."

His secret place was a giant rock out in the woods. Maybe it would have been beautiful if it were day, but the only light was from the lantern I carried. I told my mom I would never use it, but her mom senses probably had her laughing back at home, for what she thought was no apparent reason. Maxwell walked ahead of me just fine, so I assumed he could probably see in the dark.

I really had to fight the urge to grab onto his forearm while he led me. I really wanted to, like it was something I had done before. It was a very strange déjà vu, but maybe I was only being weird because I thought I was going to die horribly. "When can we stop?"

"Right here." He aimed his hand toward the big rock, which was big enough for us to both sit on and not touch. He waited for me to take my seat, and then he took his. "I'll tell you whatever you need to know. I think I owe you that."

Oh, he sure did! "Were you always a werewolf? Was Annie?"

"No. I was turned recently."

I gulped. I was afraid that was gonna be the case, which meant it wasn't an exclusive genetic thing, which meant I could turn. "By what?"

"It all started when Rich and I went to a party at a pool hall. There was this blonde Latina there who was ridiculously hot!"

I already hated her.

"She was wiping the floor with all of the guys who challenged her, and they didn't mind. It was like a privilege that she even bothered. I didn't realize that, besides her natural beauty, she was emitting pheromones that made her more appealing."

My interest was piqued.

"Rich told me to talk to her. I really wanted to, but I didn't want to bother. She gave me the impression she was a wild type, and sex was nowhere in my immediate future, so I didn't pursue her. Rich did, though, and she surprisingly gave him the time of day. They went home together. Then, he started acting strange."

"Strange?" I asked.

"He was aggressive. He was always hungry. He was suddenly a lot more ambitious, and he was obsessed with that girl. Then, he finally showed me how much stronger he had become. He let me in on his little secret and asked me if I wanted to become what he was."

"And you agreed?"

"Are you kidding me?" he screeched. "I turned him down. What kind of person would want to be a werewolf? I had that much sense before I even found out about the hunger."

"Your mother…" I really didn't want to think about her, but her body sort of left a lasting impression on me. I had never seen that much blood or open flesh. "Her body was torn apart."

"We're wolves. We'll eat anything, especially meat. We have a particular taste, though." He gulped like four times before he would quietly admit it to me. "We always eat the heart."

I didn't mean to scoot away, but I was honestly a bit uncomfortable. "And have you—?"

"I haven't hurt anyone, but Rich did. There was a girl in town that he always sort of liked, but she didn't feel the same way. He preyed on her, and he attacked her when she went for a jog early in the morning." I didn't get the impression Maxwell was a psychopath because he was expressing remorse. I could practically see the shame as it shone in his eyes. "He came to me covered in blood, asking me to help him, but I didn't want to be a part of a cover-up! When I suggested we call the police, he went nuts on me.

"He wasn't ashamed of what he had done. He was proud of it. He said it made him stronger! Rich was sweet and innocent. I didn't recognize what he had become, so I thought it was my duty to turn him in. But when I tried to leave, he bit me."

"And then what happened?"

"It didn't take long to change." He pointed to the mark on his arm. "The bite faded in a couple of minutes, and this mark of our pack appeared on my arm. I was stronger, faster, I could see better, and I had more attention from girls than I could handle."

I got sort of distracted by his bulging muscles, but at least I knew it wasn't my entire fault. "And your wolfiness is why I like you?"

"Maybe that plays a part." I was surprised he smirked. "I was freaked out, but it did seem cool at first—like I was some kind of superhero. But then, I started to get the hunger. I didn't want to hurt anyone, so I started researching about a cure."

"And the story about the pack in the U.P. is true?"

"It is, but it was also a lead given to me by Cassandra, the blonde. She mostly wanted to waste my time."

"Waste it how?"

"This form I have is something I can control, but it's the compromise between the wolf and me. When the full moon rises, I'm gonna turn completely. Once I do, it's over. There's no going back."

I frantically looked up in the sky as if I had already forgotten that it was night. It wasn't a full moon, but it looked pretty darn full to me. "When is the next full moon?"

"Three days from now."

I couldn't sit down anymore. As a matter of fact, I was straight up hyperventilating. I was pacing around and trying to calm down as if I were the one about to lose everything. "So, how do you stop it?"

"The U.P. pack told me how to do it because they thought I would back off. When I wasn't sure, they saw it as an act of betrayal to my alpha. They would have killed me if Rich wanted that to happen."

"Maxwell, what do you have to do?"

He was calm like he had made his peace about it. There was only a slight quiver in his voice. "I have to kill the person who turned me before the full moon, and I have to do it with my own two hands."

That certainly put a damper on everything. I was down for venturing off into a magical land for a rare plant and the blood of a dragon, but I wasn't expecting murder. "Are you going to do it?"

"I wasn't sure before, but I smelled him on my mother's corpse." Maxwell had to take a moment to catch his breath and stop himself from wolfing out again. "He killed her, my grandparents, and his own family! He's not the same person I grew up with. He's a monster, and I can't live like this."

He got up and started his calming pacing technique, but I felt very drained and collapsed on the rock. "Did you think about killing me? Did you think about taking a bite out of my juicy and meaty heart?"

"At first," he admitted all too casually, "but I know I don't want to kill you now."

"And why the change of heart?"

He was suddenly so embarrassed to look at me, and when he did, he really blushed. "Because I have this urge to bite you."

I scooted behind the rock and prepped myself for the most futile run of my life. "You what?"

"The wolf inside me…he wants to turn you." And he was so serious about it, too!

I rightfully began to spaz out. "I would really like not to be a werewolf. If I were a vampire, blood bags and animal blood would be gross, but not as gross as eating human hearts!"

"I actually fight my hunger by eating a lot of food and eating a couple of animals here and there."

I gasped as his freakiness became clearer. "You ate that stray, didn't you?"

"You said you wouldn't judge my cheeseburgers. Don't judge me now!"

Oh, that was not fair! Maybe if we were on the other side of the world, I wouldn't have blinked, but they were totally not the same thing in our country. "I don't want you to bite me."

"I don't want to bite you either. I think I'm just…I think we're compatible or something."

The worst part about everything (besides all the death and fear of eventually eating people) was that I hoped he was genuinely correct about the two of us and our strange connection together. It was so stupid, especially since I knew I was attracted to his pheromones, and they were making me go crazy. I didn't even smell anything! He wasn't even wearing cologne.

"Well, how are we gonna find Rich?"

"He wants me to find him. He wants me to join his pack and be his wingman. He won't be far. Maybe I could sniff him out."

I wasn't comfortable with the idea of Maxwell killing anyone, even if it were a monster. I also had doubts, considering there was only one of him and only God knew how many of them. With one bite, they could create a monster army. It was totally not cool. Everyone always had zombie apocalypse plans, but werewolves were also an epidemic!

"Maybe there's another way to save you. We should do some research. Is there a library or antique bookstore open this late?"

"Yeah, I know a place. It's about an hour's drive from here."

"Good. We need to leave before the police find us." I wouldn't know how to explain to them what happened, or to my parents when they bailed me out. "The sooner we get out of here, the better."

Chapter Six

There was a bookstore right off the interstate, but it was as big as my local library. There were a couple of strange people in there, like a goth girl who was really giving me a witch vibe. She had some creepy cat eye contacts (I assumed). There were a couple of colorful characters, like a man with an eye patch. There were also normal people as well. I mean, I was a normal person. I just happened to be traveling with a werewolf.

"Why'd you bring me here?" From the looks of things, all the fluffy teen crap I read was right up front and out in the open. "Young adult novels about cuddly werewolves that transform at will aren't gonna help us."

"The good stuff is upstairs."

I followed him up the winding staircase and—sure enough—there were tons of old books with unique bindings, and a lot of them were leather-bound. It was sort of a dream come true for a nerd like me. "I assume you checked everything obvious."

"We might as well go back over everything again."

"Let's be creative. Let's look at ancient warriors, particularly Spaniards or Aztecs. You said she was Latina."

"And what else?"

"Curses. They must have changed somehow."

We started our search. There were a couple of books on supernatural creatures, but werewolf stuff was just typical lore. According to the legends, werewolves were infected after a bite or sometimes a scratch. They would transform during full moons and become uncontrollable beasts that would kill anything they could find. Consumption of the heart was mentioned a couple of times, but wolves were known for being greedy things. They had heightened senses, super strength, and were fiercely loyal to one another. Their only real weakness was silver and wolfsbane.

"Is the silver thing real?"

"I'm not allergic to it, but if you stab me in the heart with anything, or blow my brains out, I assume I'm going to die."

"That's good to know."

His eyes widened.

"No. Not good! I mean, it's nice to know how to kill you—not you! I mean, Rich." I laughed nervously. He only got more offended and angrier the more I talked. "I don't wanna kill your friend, it's just important to—"

"Stop. Count to three. Start again."

I took a deep breath and counted in my head. Three…two…one. "And is wolfsbane poisonous to you?"

"It's poisonous to everyone, but I assume I would be more likely to survive if I ingested it than you."

I sighed. "Well, these legends are useless. We already know you're not bound by a full moon. Your form before a full moon is scary and vicious enough."

"Yeah. I'm just a vicious and scary animal."

"That's so not what I mean!" I really hated that I had no idea how to communicate with people. "This curse isn't bound to the moon. There's more to this story, or it's evolved."

Poor Maxwell was becoming impatient. He was about to change into something he couldn't control, and we didn't know how to stop it, other than stopping his seemingly unstoppable friend. It was all very complicated.

I tried to turn to my computer for help, but it was difficult connecting to the web. When I was connected, it was slow. "The Wi-Fi in here sucks!"

Maxwell was amused by me, for whatever strange reason, and he smiled a little bit. "Why are you doing this?"

"Doing what?"

"Helping me."

I shrugged. I assumed I was doing it because I was a good person, but maybe there was some crazy mixed in there, too. But when I thought about it, I guess I had a reason. "Because we're somehow connected, and I don't know if this has anything to do with werewolf lore or Fate pulling us back together. I need to separate what's real and what's not, and this is the only way I know to do it."

His eyes were drawn to my shaking and glowing phone on the table. "Your parents are calling again?"

"I keep texting them that I'm fine, but I don't think they know how to read it."

He chuckled. "But they can track your car?"

"Isn't that ridiculous?" They were such strange people, but I guess having two children kidnapped and one murdered, would do that to you. I couldn't imagine their pain, but I wished they had let me know, so I could have helped them.

"What are you looking for?" He came around the table and sat close to me, which threw me off a little bit. Our faces were sort of close. I had to remind myself that now wasn't the time to make him vomit with a kiss.

"Well, there are plenty of cultures that believe consuming human hearts gives them power: Native American Tribes, Aztecs, Spaniards, Africans, and I wouldn't be surprised if we found some Viking mythology, too. Maybe those practices are somehow tied into werewolfism—if that's a word."

"What's it matter if it's a word? It's a thing."

"True." I really was having a hard time not falling for his pheromone thing. I didn't know how I was supposed to fight against it. All my brain power was fighting for him, so I couldn't just turn it around to fight to not have him.

"That's smart. I didn't think about that when I was researching."

"What did you look up?"

"Something like, 'Are werewolves real?' From there, I let the freak show in, I guess." We both laughed. I could only imagine what he found. "It pays off to know sick little girls."

I pouted, and I'm sure I looked rather childish. "I'm a woman!"

"Yeah, I noticed." Oh boy, I think he was noticing. He was staring at me all longingly, and it might have been my imagination, but I think he was leaning in toward me. I think I accidentally did that lip bite thing I wasn't supposed to do, but he didn't get mad. He smirked like he was attracted to me.

I decided to just go for it, but he did flinch. I pulled away before I made contact. "I'm sorry."

"I'm the one who should be sorry." He took a deep breath and moved back across the table. He didn't look well, but instead of being pale, all the blood was sort of rushing to his face like he was in a very intense fight with himself. He even had a vein popping out of his head. "This is unfair to you. It's chemistry and magic."

"Alchemy."

"Yeah, I guess so." He buried his nose in a book we had already looked through, to pretend not to be awkward, but we totally were. I think we were both a little worried about his urge to bite me as well. I wasn't crazy enough to want him to, and there weren't enough pheromones in the world to make me either.

But what if he did bite me? I didn't know Maxwell incredibly well, but I think I knew him well enough to know he was a gentleman. He would probably want me to kill him in order to stop the transformation. That way, I could be a human, and he'd never live long enough to be a monster.

I had to stop thinking like that. Knowing my luck, I was going to will that sort of destiny into existence.

I continued researching. I looked up tales of lycanthropy and its origins, other than pop culture. Of course, I found something in Greek mythology. "Have you heard of Lycaon?"

Maxwell shook his head.

"He was transformed into a wolf after ritually killing a child. Zeus cursed him for his crimes."

"Okay, but that's just a legend."

"Yeah, but legends get their start from somewhere. There are at least three more Greek stories like this. And werewolves are cannibals."

"Not technically. I'm not a human anymore..." He mumbled, embarrassed. I honestly couldn't blame him. I didn't like telling people I was obsessed with pinto beans, so I certainly wouldn't want to brag about craving people.

"So, you think werewolves are somehow cursed by the gods for eating people, and now they have to live as beasts that crave people?" He didn't have to get so snippy about it.

"When you say it like that, it sounds silly, but maybe the curse was meant to bring out what the gods already thought they were. Maybe it wasn't one pagan god. Maybe it was a league that banded together."

"Zeus and Odin must have decided to curse the sickest murderers over tea."

"Maybe it was one god...like God himself! I don't know, but it's obviously supernatural. This is a curse, and if you can only break it by killing your sire before the full moon rises, it's purely mystical."

"So, what should I do? Should I go pray in a church? Should I find the most violent of warlords, ask them if they pissed off a deity, and if we can give them a bottle of wine to kiss and make up?"

"Maybe that would work if you could pull off a decent kiss," I mumbled.

I got a pretty fierce glare from him. "That's not very funny right now."

It wasn't, and yet, I struggled to keep my laugh in. "Do you think being kidnapped has anything to do with this?"

"I didn't. Rich was bitten first. He had nothing to do with it. I thought trouble was just following me. I thought I was cursed because I was just cursed."

"But you and I are quite a coincidence." It was hard not to press my mysterious past, but I had to be careful. I mean, he was traumatized. "Was Annie…eaten?"

I thought he would go ballistic, but he got real quiet and still. Then, he took a deep breath and closed the book. "They found a couple of the children's bodies, but they never found Annie's or your brother's."

I didn't realize I was trembling. I had to hold my arms to keep myself still. I could feel something was wrong. It was like a little shiver of terror from when my dog scratched at the door of my room. He was supposed to protect me, but all I felt was pure terror. "Then why do we think they're dead?"

"The blood. There was too much blood." It wasn't all blocked out. He remembered something, and if it wasn't all coherent, then he could at least feel what it felt like.

"But maybe—"

"I know you don't remember your brother, but I remember Annie quite well." Maxwell became very intense, and his eyes began to change. "I remember what it was like to lose her, and I remember burying her empty coffin knowing that she was gone. I've accepted it. Let it go."

"Okay." I was not okay, but I buried my head in another book. I don't think he realized how intimidating he suddenly was with the seething and the groaning. It made me very uncomfortable.

We did find some more stories about violent cultures in more detail. The Spaniards received a lot of influence from Rome, and the

Romans were famous for their brutal coliseum battles. I could see someone snacking on a heart before a big battle, especially if they thought it would give them enough strength to survive another day. We didn't honestly find any answers, but we had plenty of questions afterward.

We couldn't stay too long in the bookstore. We were kicked out a little bit after ten, but I bought a book, so we wouldn't be rude. I didn't know where to drive to exactly, so we sat in the car for a while. "Should we stay in a local hotel? It would be weird considering how close you are to home. It might raise questions about what happened."

"No one has to know that I'm here. I'll lay low."

I was sort of surprised he wanted to stick around. More specifically, I was surprised he wanted to stick around *with* me. I wouldn't question it. I let him guide me to a cute motel that was pretty much like an old mansion. It totally had a horror movie vibe I was trying to avoid, and it didn't help that I knew a pack of werewolves was potentially after me.

I did buy two rooms. I knew Maxwell didn't want me to pay for it, but it would have been much more awkward sharing a room together. We got our keys from the manager and went upstairs. I handed Maxwell his key when we got to his door. "This is your room, I guess."

"Right next to yours?" He almost laughed nervously, but it was cute that Maxwell was nervous.

"That's good! What if monsters try to kill me?"

"It's best I'm near." He nodded a couple of times and shifted from his heels to his toes.

Knowing how bad I was at everything, and considering that contact with me literally revolted him, made me just wanna get in the shower and sleep. "Goodnight."

"Goodnight."

I stepped inside. It was quite the suite. There were all sorts of creepy souvenirs that were going to give me nightmares, including a stuffed eagle. I didn't know if I was going to be able to sleep, or if my fear of the eagle springing to life and ripping off my face with its talons was going to come true.

I noticed there were three doors. One was to my bathroom, which was surprisingly spotless and practically sparkling. There was the door I just walked through, but the third was poking at my brain. I unlocked the door and opened it. There was another door behind the door, and Maxwell opened it only seconds after I opened mine. "Our rooms are conjoining."

"Yeah, I see."

Well, I wasn't tired anymore. I was thinking about him being a door away from me, and all the uncertainties I needed to know. "Come in for a minute."

I stepped away to give him the space to walk in. Last time we were alone in a hotel room, I tried to put the moves on him. My heart was beating like I was gonna try it. I had to keep reminding myself he wouldn't like that, and I would only end up severely embarrassed. "I think what you're doing is brave. I just thought you needed to know."

"Thank you. It hasn't been easy resisting the urge to hurt someone."

Well, that kind of broke my romantic mood. "But you do have to hurt someone if you want to become a human again."

By the instant lack of color on his face, I realized I broke his mood, too. That was sort of unbelievable. He must have thought about it by now.

"How are you going to do that if you can't touch someone? Your fear cripples you."

I didn't want to think about Maxwell killing his former best friend, but I would have rather seen him come out alive in the final battle. I wanted to grab Maxwell by his shoulders and shake some sense into him, but he wouldn't move. "I need you to find a way to fight him, but you can't even hold my hand without turning a little green."

"I can do it if I have to—"

"How?" He was lying to me. He totally was. I sort of hyperventilated, because he was so going to die. Then, something awful was going to happen to me. I just knew it!

"Just calm down a little bit. Wait a moment." He closed his eyes and took a deep breath. He took a few seconds and opened them. His wolfie eyes were different, but they were kind of cool. They were yellowish, but brown-tinted—I guess more golden. They were wild, but totally calm, like he knew everything about the world, and he was ready to do anything about it. It's hard to explain exactly, but I knew it was kind of hot.

"I can feel the wolf. I know it sounds stupid, but I can." His fingers twitched a little bit before he moved his hand toward me. I almost gasped, but I kept myself quiet. I didn't wanna ruin our first intimate moment together. His fingers only grazed mine, and we didn't really hold hands—our fingertips cupped with each other—but it was amazing. It was hope, and it was electrifying. "He's not afraid of anything, and I know if I embraced him, I would be unstoppable."

It was nice if we decided to engage in a relationship, it wouldn't be pointless, but I was concerned. I mean, he did say he wanted to bite me, and he had his wolf eyes on. What if his teeth popped out? I didn't wanna be like him, even if I really wanted him. "I know you feel like I'm attracted to you because you're a wolf—maybe I am—but I do know you're a very sweet guy on your own."

I watched his transition back to normal, and his hand pulled away from me. He even wiped my touch away on his pants furiously. "A sweet guy isn't going to kill his best friend."

"Your family was murdered. I'm not exactly comfortable with all of this, but I promise I won't judge."

"You certainly are a special girl." For someone smiling, he was certainly very sad. "I think I'm gonna go back to my room, but I'll keep my eye on you."

"We're safe here, right? You don't sense Rich coming to eat my heart out, do you?"

"I wouldn't let anything happen to you, Jesse. I promise."

Usually, those declarations were met with tender or passionate kisses. I had to settle for a steely gaze. It made me believe him. He had the hero look down to a science. "I trust you."

"Goodnight." He started to leave, but he turned and gave me this little smirk before he walked through his door. Maxwell was totally hot, and he was being subtly sexy about it. Maybe it was him. Maybe it was the wolf luring me into his den of iniquity.

I lay in my bed for a while, wondering what was going to happen between the two of us. Maxwell only had three days left. He was either going to be a killer or a werewolf. I wondered if he was going to end up okay as either one, and I wondered why I was still determined to crush on him either way.

Chapter Seven

I woke up early in the morning. I guess it was hard to think about Maxwell having so little time left. I didn't wanna bother him if he was sleeping. He deserved some rest.

I did wanna learn more about the kidnapping, and he was only a little kid when it happened. I figured the internet should be able to tell me more than his traumatized mind. When I tried to search for my name, I didn't find anything about it. I guess they didn't really promote child kidnappings on the top search engines, but I expected something after combing page after page. I mean, it's not like I had anything else to contribute to society other than a couple of selfies.

I tried Maxwell's name, and the story popped right up. My name was mentioned in the article, but I didn't recognize it. It said: "Jessica Rossen." That was so not my name. I didn't understand what right my parents had to change our entire family's name, unless there was more to the story I didn't know. Well, of course, there was more to the story, but it made me believe they were keeping secrets from me about an assassin chasing after us.

Anyway, the articles said Maxwell, Annie, my brother, and I were taken and missing for three days, along with other children from various cities. I was found wandering on the side of the road, and a concerned family brought me to a police station. I told the police that Maxwell helped me out, and I led them to finding him. Our siblings' bodies and most of the children were never found, but there was so much blood that they were certain none of them survived. The kidnappers were never found, but after two months of searching, they and the ten other children were proclaimed dead.

No wonder why I felt like I could trust Maxwell. I subconsciously knew that I could. "Maxwell?" I knocked on his door and waited a while. I became impatient and opened my door. I was surprised when I saw that his was open, and no one was inside. "Maxwell?"

The bathroom door was wide open, but I walked inside of it to check the shower. I wasn't hoping I would catch him in the act of anything, but I was disappointed he wasn't there. His backpack and jacket were missing as well.

Then, I checked the little notepad that hotels leave on your desk. He left me a note.

Jesse,

It was amazing seeing you again and getting to know the woman you became. I never believed in Fate before, but whatever this is, I don't want you caught up in it any longer. I wouldn't be able to live with myself if you were harmed because of me. Your parents don't deserve the sort of pain I remember they went through when your brother died.

Please be safe, and don't bother to look for me. I don't want you to see what I'll become, one way or another.

Good luck on your journey. I know you'll make a wonderful doctor, just like Kevin wanted to be.

Maxwell

I collapsed on his bed and pouted for a little while. He did the noble thing by walking away from me. I should have never gotten involved. Besides, if he turned back into a human, I'm sure he would have looked me up in Arizona. Why wouldn't he?

I gathered my things together and left. I didn't wanna stick around while I moped and wondered if he would change his mind. I shouldn't have wanted him to either. I should have allowed him to keep what human decency he had left.

I wondered if I was a colossal jerk for packing up and leaving right away. Should I have given him like ten minutes to reconsider? Thirty minutes? A day?

Just for good measure, I did eat breakfast in the dining room, and I ate very slowly. After I finished, I figured it was enough time to let him reflect (especially since it took so long to get my food).

I saw my dad called me like thirty-seven times, and he even tried to video chat with me. Since he made that monumental effort, I went ahead and answered his call. "Hi, Dad."

"Why have you been ignoring us?"

"Because you were calling Jesse Holloway, and my name is Jessica Rossen."

Dad silently gasped. Then, he was deafeningly quiet for a couple of agonizingly long seconds. "Sweetheart—"

"Do I even know your real names?"

"No. You don't."

I thought I was just confused about my life, but it turned out that I was actually very angry and completely betrayed. "I can't believe you've kept this huge secret from me."

"What happened to you and your brother was so painful, and we didn't want you to live with those scars. We gave you a new name and a new home, so we could have a fresh start."

The worst part about it all was that I felt like a jerk for not remembering my brother. I was an even greater traitor than my parents because I didn't even have enough sense to miss him. "I don't even know who I was. How am I supposed to figure out who I am?"

"I think you've got a pretty good idea, Jesse. You make us so proud every day." I could hear Dad's voice rasping as he struggled to speak through his emotions. "It's hard for us to let go, but I know it's important. You're gonna do great things."

I wanted to, but I seemed like such a small person to myself. I didn't think I was much of a smear on the pages of destiny. I bet my brother would have been different. He seemed to really impact Maxwell, even though they were only little kids. "Do you ever still wonder about Kevin? Do you ever question if he's alive?"

"Every morning when I wake up, I pray to God he's somehow alive. By the time I hit my pillow at night, I pray he's gone. Wanting him here with me may be selfish. After everything he went through, it's a better comfort knowing he's in the arms of angels."

"It would be better than the alternative," I mumbled to myself.

"What do you mean?"

"Nothing!" If I even began to explain my working theory of being kidnapped by werewolves as a child, he would have sent a medical team to meet me when I arrived at my dorm. "I'm sorry I can't remember him. Do you remember the other children who were taken?"

"I do, but mostly their parents. We don't keep in contact now."

I considered telling them about Maxwell, but we were already having a conversation that shouldn't have taken place on a phone. "I have to drive in one of those roundabout things, so I need to concentrate. I'll call you back later."

"Alright, sweetheart." He hung up the phone after he caught the hint. I didn't mean to lie. I just really didn't know what else to say.

I stopped at a gas station to pee, and then I pumped a little bit more gas. There was no point in ending up in the middle of nowhere with an empty tank.

While I was pumping, I saw a girl walking around. She was really pretty, like she could have been a model. She didn't seem like the sort of person who should have been traveling alone, but I guess I was also traveling alone…

She spotted me and walked over while carrying a folded map in her hand. "Hi. I'm a little lost. I was hoping you could tell me how to get back on the interstate."

"I can't!" I laughed like a nerd, "but I'm sure my GPS could tell you." I took my phone out of my purse and opened my map app.

"Thank you." She was gorgeous, and she had a little something going on. She didn't look purely Caucasian like I did. She spoke with a perfect Midwest accent. "I'm just passing through, so I'm unfamiliar with the territory."

"Well, if you're anything like me, then you have no idea where you're going in new places!"

"Well, I have no real worries." She smirked, and her accent changed, like into a real accent. "I usually follow my nose, and I've been chasing a particular scent."

"Oh…?" I gulped and took a step back. The only other person around in the area was the cashier in the gas station, and she was blocking me and my car. I guess there was always the chance I was misinterpreting what she meant, but I got the feeling I was justified in being completely terrified. "You're a werewolf, aren't you?"

"I am." She was that hot Latina Maxwell told me about! I feared her werewolfiness, but I think I was just a tad more intimidated by her physique, which was insane. "And you're Max's little pet, aren't you?"

"He doesn't like to be called 'Max,' and I'm not a pet."

"Doesn't matter what you are." She grabbed my braid and rubbed the tip of it with her fingers. "You're soon to be bait for Maxwell's wonderful return to our pack."

"No. I won't let you use me like this." I pulled away from her and bolted. I ran back into the gas station to find something to fight her off with. Maybe I could distract her with a toy bone or something, but Rich was inside. I recognized him from Maxwell's pictures, and he was standing over the poor cashier, who had his skull bashed in.

"Hey." He was so calm—happy even—when he saw me. "You're cute. I see why Maxwell digs you."

Then, he tried to touch me with his bloodied fingers! "Stay away from me."

He laughed like I was an insane person for being terrified of him. "I'm afraid I can't do that. You see, Maxwell knows good and well that he should join me. We're like brothers. Just because I'm his sire, alpha, and a genuine monster shouldn't get in the way of that. We've been friends for too long to let something like food tear us apart."

"Humans. People. You used to be one." There had to be a way to appeal to his inner goodness. Maybe after eating all those hearts, he'd remember he had one.

"And I'm not anymore. Neither is he." He shook his head at me in disbelief. Rich just couldn't understand why I couldn't see. "Should I turn you as well?"

"I think you should give Maxwell some time to do it," the girl said from behind. "I think he'll break."

"My woman believes he'll break." They were so sick. He had such satisfaction thinking about corrupting poor Maxwell. I wished I could have smacked that smug smile right off his face! "Let's see."

His fist came at me so quickly, I didn't even see it coming. I didn't even feel it until I woke up in some sort of metal structure on a bed of old blankets. My head was pounding, and that's not even an expression. It literally felt like someone was beating me in the face repeatedly. I touched my cheek where it hurt the most, and it felt puffy. I probably looked like a freak.

I was alone for a little while before Cassandra and Rich came waltzing in like they owned the place. Well, maybe they did, but only because they probably ate whoever used to. "Where am I?"

"Our stomping grounds," Rich admitted shamelessly. "We'll probably move out once we complete our pack."

I looked around, and I wasn't exactly impressed. It was dark and dingy where they were holding me. It was also very hollow and roundish. "Maxwell wants to be human. He'll never join with you."

"There is no turning back!" he laughed. "There's no cure for him or any of us, so he might as well accept the gift I've given him."

I gave him a moment to rephrase his statement, but he meant to sound incredibly insane. "Killing his family was a gift?"

"They're not his family. I'm his family." The worst part about his craziness was that he believed it. Rich was offended that I couldn't understand, and that Maxwell just couldn't see it. "And frankly, you'll be an unsuitable mate if you don't turn as well."

"I don't wanna be his mate. I barely know him!" Nobody was that hot!

"But he's captured your heart nonetheless." Cassandra placed her hands on her chest and pretended to swoon. "How does Maxwell do it so fast?"

"With being terrified to touch a woman? I have no idea." For an alpha, he sure did sound jealous.

"Did you kill your family?"

"My parents, but my siblings saw the light once I bit them." There wasn't even a tiny shred of remorse coming from him. It's not like he might have hated his parents, and it satisfied him to know they were gone. He literally thought nothing of them. "You'll see as well."

I shook my head slowly back and forth. Then, he was even more amazed and confused than I was.

"You think you truly like this normal life you're living? Do you think it's fulfilling to be a nothing passing through time? It's not. It's humiliating, and it's pointless. Open your eyes and see."

I awkwardly shrugged my shoulders. "I see just fine."

He angrily grunted and pushed me to the ground. "You're weak. You're slow. You're terrified. What if you could be strong? What if you could be a standout? You wouldn't want that?"

I had enough sense to know I shouldn't upset him, but I didn't know how not to do that exactly. "I know I don't wanna kill people."

"You only think it's wrong because you're a human. It's different for me. I see most of you as food."

I was near tears at this point. "And am I food?"

"No. You're the girl my friend wants to mate with, and I think I should give you to him as a gift. When he finds you, he'll turn you."

I was so furious at him. I didn't know how long he would have me, but I wanted to get under his skin. "There is a cure. If Maxwell can kill his sire before the full moon, he can return to normal."

He laughed at first, but when he realized my steely gaze had a solid foundation, and his lady friend wasn't laughing along, he wasn't so cocky anymore. "Is this true?" he asked her.

She sighed heavily. "It is. You and I have much to discuss."

He certainly became very angry. I just got the feeling Rich wasn't as in charge as he thought. "Then let's go discuss."

I couldn't believe they left me, but they did. I wasn't chained down to anything. I tried for the door, but that was locked. I didn't have many ideas. I wasn't an escape artist. I couldn't even change my own tire!

I sat down with my legs folded and tried to think about how to overcome Rich and Cassandra. I needed to get away before they somehow forced Maxwell to bite me. There was no going back after that. Even if I did somehow like being a wolf and wanted to be with him, I think Maxwell would have felt too guilty to embrace us. He was my protector, after all. He saved me all those years ago. He would try to save me again.

And all that stuff Rich said was just downright offensive! I was not a nothing passing through time. I had parents who loved me, and I was on my way to becoming a doctor. It was gonna take a couple of years, but I was gonna save lives. Then, I was gonna meet a nice boy, settle down, and have babies. I think I could manage a career and children, but I'd cross that bridge when I got there. Maybe my perfect man would stay home and take care of the babies.

Oh, but then again, I didn't know if I was ready to face the social stigma that came with that sort of dynamic. It was weird. I didn't need to be a breadwinner. I just wanted to be a doctor.

Oh! I could be one of those doctors without borders. I didn't need money. I just wanted to save lives and do the most good. Boom! There. Problem solved. I would marry a fellow doctor who would support me in my decision.

But…I didn't solve the kid dilemma though…

That didn't matter! I didn't have everything figured out, but that's because I was a young human. I had loads of time to sort all my thoughts out. I was gonna do stuff and make a difference.

Eventually, I heard metal clanking continuously. It was happening so fast; I was afraid for my safety. I got up and ran as far away as I could from the door, but that didn't really matter. I didn't have anywhere to run when Rich came bursting through the door, yelling his head off, with wolfie eyes and fangs. "You think it's so simple, don't you? You wait here to be rescued, and Maxwell kills me and receives salvation?"

"Something like that." I winced as he quickly came up on me and loomed. I was kidnapped and stalked by a genuine monster. I'm surprised all I did was whimper like a coward, and not pee on myself like a complete loser.

I felt his hot breath, and his growls didn't really help calm the fear, but he did take a few deep breaths and, eventually, began to laugh.

I slowly looked up. There was definitely nothing funny going on. There was no reason for him to have a villain laugh!

Rich grabbed my braid and felt its silky texture until he was bored enough to let it fall on my shoulder. He smirked and took a step closer, but I couldn't move away unless I phased through the wall. I so did not want to be around that psychopath. "What if Maxwell had to make a noble sacrifice? What if it were his humanity or yours?"

I took a deep breath, and I had a queasy feeling in my stomach like it would be my last. "What do you mean?"

He grabbed my shoulders and thrust me against the wall. I looked over his shoulder and saw Cassandra smiling deviously. I wondered if she knew when she turned Rich that this would happen. I mean, she probably didn't figure me into her plans. I was just a pawn in her little game, but she must have known she could lure Maxwell there somehow. And if she always planned to have Maxwell, then what was she planning on doing with Rich?

"No! No! No!" He opened his mouth, and his fangs expanded and sank right through my flesh. I was sure he was going to take a chunk right out of my shoulder, but he had enough control to release his grasp as soon as the contamination was complete.

It hurt. I mean, it really hurt! A lot. I don't remember really processing all the pain, because I was afraid of what would happen to me. Tears streamed down my face, and snot poured into my mouth. I stuttered out words that didn't make sense. It was just terrible ramblings of a mad woman.

I held my bloodied arm and watched the teeth marks. As long as I was wounded, with blood seeping out like a cherry fountain, I'd be human. I didn't wanna stop being human!

Then, the bleeding just stopped. I tried squeezing my right shoulder to aggravate the wound, but the holes inside of me were closed, and I was so doomed. "What have you done to me?"

I slid down to the floor sobbing, but Rich bent down to pour salt in my wounds with a satisfied and sadistic grin. "Either you'll have to kill me, or he will. One of you will have to stay a werewolf, and the other will live their life normally. But if you two are drawing each other together, then something tells me you'll both be howling at the moon, with the rest of us, very soon."

There wasn't even a little bit of sympathy from either of them. There was no remorse. I bet he'd honestly expected me to feel grateful for what he had done to me. Well, he was gonna be sorry he had ever touched me! "You will pay for this."

"Is that you talking or your wolf, because you don't strike me as the type of girl who would normally resort to threats." I hated that he laughed at my heightened emotions. I was really angry. I had a reason, but I didn't feel like myself. I could feel my heart pumping through my throbbing head and shaking ears. I could hear it, and it wasn't slowing down.

"Let her cool down, Rich. We have a guest to prepare for."

The reminder only made him smile even more. "Soon, our pack will be complete."

I really hated him, but I knew I wasn't strong enough to fight him. I wanted to escape, but I didn't have anywhere to go if Maxwell didn't find me. I didn't know how to live as a monster.

Again, they left me alone. I tried to be strong in front of them (even though I cried and freaked out a lot), but I couldn't hold my composure now. I collapsed into the hardest and heaviest cry of my life. In two days, I would permanently be a heart-craving monster. I couldn't have a future or be with my parents again if I were a danger. But at least I loved them enough to care. I was afraid he would take that away from me. I was afraid I would change and become like him.

All I could hope for was for Maxwell to save me, but if he did, it would mean the end of my humanity, or his.

Chapter Eight

I was trapped in my prison for the remainder of the night. I cried myself to sleep. Then, I picked up where I left off in the morning. Cassandra eventually barged in and growled when she saw I was still on the floor, sniffling. "Are you honestly still crying?"

I pouted and looked up at her in disbelief. What else was I supposed to do? "Your alpha bit me!"

She laughed. "He's your alpha. He's not mine."

I wiped my eyes, but I never planned to stop crying about being a monster. "What is that supposed to mean?"

She came and sat next to me like we were supposed to be best friends. "It means I'm the girl you wanna talk to."

I wanted to move away from her, but I was afraid of offending her. It was stupid, but I knew she was impossibly strong, and I didn't stand a chance. It was more than just my fear. It was complete rationality embedded in my DNA. "You started this."

"I did." She was so smug about it, too.

I really wanted to slap her or something, but I was still too timid. I knew she was the bad guy of the story, though. I could just feel it in my gut. "You wanted Maxwell first. Why? Did you have anything to do with us being kidnapped when we were younger?"

She seemed confused. "Were you there?"

Oh, geez! It occurred to me that I probably shouldn't have said anything about my mysterious past with Maxwell.

"You were the girl who escaped?" She laughed from excitement, and that really freaked me out. "How wild is it that you just happened to fall right back into Maxwell's life? Wow! Fate sure is something."

But she proved to me that she was really watching Maxwell. And if she knew about his past, then maybe she was responsible. "Did you have anything to do with my brother's death?"

I got really scared because I had honestly offended her. "Of course, I didn't, and neither did the pack I came from. We're a lot of things, but kidnappers and baby eaters aren't one of them."

She calmed down and pretended like she was going to bite me. "A child isn't nearly as delicious anyway."

I crawled away on my hands and knees as soon as her fangs started reaching for my neck. "Get away from me!"

Cassandra laughed again and walked to me, swaying her hips, as if I were a man and she was trying to seduce me. "Don't freak out on me, sweetheart! I wanna help you with your transition."

I looked at the door. If I were fast enough, there was a chance I could reach it before she ripped my heart out. "I don't want your kind of help."

"You don't mean that."

"I do." I had to be brave. I bolted as fast as I could for the door that was probably locked, so I could fight my way past probably a dozen guards. I didn't care. I needed some sort of hope! But I don't even know if I took three steps before Cassandra tossed me into the metal wall by my neck. I bounced right off it and landed on the ground. I thought I was snapped in two, but when I tried to wiggle my toes to check, I felt my whole body scream.

"We can fight it out if you want, but I'm still gonna take you out." Cassandra was very relaxed about the delivery of her threat, but there was just enough hardcoreness that I knew she would really hurt me if she needed to.

"Fine."

I was determined to stay with my nose pressed against my metal prison, but she pulled me to my feet as I weighed as much as a feather. "Let's get you cleaned up."

When she opened the door I had been eyeing like a hawk, the sun poured in. There weren't any guards waiting outside. All I could see was a balcony that wrapped around my prison and a ladder. I guess it finally made sense that they felt comfortable leaving me alone unguarded. I didn't realize I was hovering so high off the ground in a water tower.

"Come on, wimp. We've got stuff to do." She fearlessly slid down the rails of the ladder as if she had experience on a pole at a fire station—or a gentlemen's club. I didn't even wanna climb down at all, and she decided to be so blatantly reckless.

I didn't want to be a prisoner, but I also didn't want to risk my life and climb down. I was so uncoordinated. One slip, and it was all over for me. I didn't wanna die as a transitioning werewolf. How would God feel about that? Was there like even a real place for me to go?

"Don't make me wait!" Cassandra yelled. "You can't afford to waste any more of your life!"

I huffed out a big amount of air. I was totally insulted. I was not wasting my life prior. I hadn't accomplished much, but everything I did was building up to a long life of helping people. I didn't deserve to be belittled by those mongrels. "Fine!"

I was still very terrified. I made the terrible decision of looking down first, so I had to take another moment to kind of catch my breath. They obviously needed me, or their little plan wouldn't work. Cassandra wasn't going to let me die, so I wasn't going to fall.

My shaky hands grabbed the rails, and I slowly stepped on each step and felt a little bit more terrified with each one, even though I was getting closer to the ground. About midway, I was finally too petrified to continue any further, and I was certainly too chicken to go back up. "Why did you make me do this?"

"Just let go!" I heard the voice of a man I didn't recognize. I made the mistake of looking down and saw a crowd of people just staring up at me. I didn't want an audience to peer-pressure me into more stuff I didn't wanna do. We were not a fraternity. They freaking kidnapped me!

"Leave me alone!" I closed my eyes and gripped the rails tighter. I knew I couldn't stay there all day, but I was safer dangling for my life than joining the rabid dog people below.

"Move out of the way." I peeked down and saw Rich pushing through the crowd and making his way to the ladder. I realized I was wearing a dress. It wasn't very short, but that was irrelevant when he was climbing underneath me.

"Oh, no! Gross. Go away!" I started to climb back up the ladder to get away, but I didn't get too far with that either. I closed my eyes and pressed my forehead against the ladder in embarrassment and shame. "Don't look up my dress!"

"If you've got something I haven't seen before, then we should probably get it looked at. We don't need it mutating with the transformation."

I gasped at his crude comment while the dogs below laughed at me. I pulled on my dress to tighten it, but I could only do so much with one hand while I was terrified of falling off. He forcibly flung me over his shoulder and started climbing down. I was a screaming mess right in his ear, so he eventually let go of the ladder and let gravity do the rest of the work. I screamed some more, but we were back on the ground pretty quickly.

"That wasn't so bad, was it?"

I pushed myself off him, and in my rage, I punched his chest. He was laughing about it, and that infuriated me even more. How could he treat me so horribly and be okay with it? I was one of his pack, wasn't I? And you don't treat women like that! "You are such a pig!"

"No, I'm a wolf." He crept up on me, smiling, and he had very flirty eyes like I was supposed to stop feeling so angry about everything. Unfortunately, I did. I don't know why, but I really couldn't hurt him. I felt an odd sense of…loyalty to him. That really sucked. "Stand down, little wolf."

"I'm not one of you."

"Really?" He grabbed my shoulder and showed me the spot where he had bitten me. His teeth marks were long gone, but the same mark that was on Maxwell was suddenly on me. "This is the mark of my pack. Everyone here has one. This is how I know who serves under me." He pulled the collar of his shirt down, so I could see the mark on his shoulder. It was like mine but more detailed. "This is the mark of the alpha. If you defeat me, it's yours. If you can't, fall in line."

No way did I feel like I could beat him. Everyone was watching me like they expected I would try or something, kind of like they were holding their breath in anticipation. I didn't know if they were gonna let me attack their leader or if they were gonna eat my heart out to stop me. I didn't get those crazy wolves. "I just want to go to college and be a doctor."

"That life is over." He was so proud of himself and how he had ruined my entire life! "I've given you a chance to embrace your true self. Peek into the beast that you know you are."

He looked to his pack, and one by one, they all knelt before their leader. It was a bit dramatic, but my heart was beating so rapidly, I could feel it in my throat. I really thought I was gonna swallow it and die. My knees shook, and I wanted to bow. I didn't feel like there was a reason not to, even though I could spout them out in French, Spanish, or Japanese. Cassandra wasn't bowing, and she wasn't going to. She watched everything go down with a smile on her face.

"You are a stubborn one." He grabbed my arm and began to squeeze. I started to scream, but I shut my mouth tight and dimmed it down to a whimper. He was hurting me, and he didn't seem to care either. "You think these humans will welcome you back once they know you crave their hearts? There's nowhere to go. You should embrace your new family."

I looked to Cassandra to get a reading on what I should do, but all she had to offer me was a smirk and a curious eyebrow.

"Cassandra isn't the leader of my pack. Don't look to her to find out what to do." He didn't sound very angry, but I knew he was threatening me. "Submit, Jesse."

He reached out his other hand toward me, and I stepped back in fear. It became clear to me that I wasn't going to fight him, and he would be willing to hurt me to make me kneel. Did that make him a pig, or did that make him an equal opportunist? "I just wanna go home."

"You'll do as I say, Jesse." He was still smiling, but I continually felt his threat surging all around me. He was seriously about to engage in a fight I was nowhere near ready for.

I took a deep breath, and my knees buckled. I didn't think too much about it until they hit the dirt. I looked up at him, horrified and amazed at myself. I knew as plain as day that I did not want this man to lead me. I could not forget that he ruined my life. But for some reason, I was growing attached to him.

"Now, are you really waiting for Maxwell to come and kill me?"

"I am." I was surprised I spoke up, considering how frightened I was of Rich.

He narrowed his eyes in on me. "And you think he can defeat me?"

"I know he can." I had no proof. What I knew about Maxwell's phobia should have led me to believe the opposite, but I could sense he was tough. He was definitely alpha material.

"Interesting…" Rich was a little ticked off—that was for certain—but I could see he was also intrigued by the challenge. "I'll make him submit, Jesse. Don't get any twisted fantasies about your boyfriend taking over my pack and ruling as their queen."

"I don't have any fantasies about Maxwell."

He laughed and turned to Cassandra. "It's amusing how high the level of denial is on this girl."

"Why don't you stop playing god and let me teach her a thing or two?" The more I saw them interact, the more I could see how bored she was with Rich. "Your little plot to make Maxwell one of us may not work if she's a housebroken slave. Let's make her strong."

The sad thing was that Rich had no idea Cassandra had some sort of secret agenda going on. It was very impressive that she had him under her thumb without even lifting a finger. "She's all yours."

He abandoned me to go hang out with some of the boys. I assumed they were going to do something chauvinistic while Cassandra was gonna dress me up like some kind of doll for Maxwell. I had no interest in playing a role in her dastardly plans, but I didn't exactly know how to escape. At that point, I was too afraid to try.

Their base was an abandoned mill, but they mostly wanted to play outside. I guess it was a wolf thing. I could smell something amazing, though, almost like when Dad cooked barbecue outside on the grill. We walked by two girls sitting on a balcony eating what looked like burgers. My stomach started rumbling like it was gonna cave in on itself. I hadn't eaten since I was at that hotel, but it was weird that I would be willing to eat meat. "Is there normal food here?"

She thought that was a funny question for some reason. "Werewolves can eat the same diet as a normal human. We crave hearts, though. You'll never live without consuming one. There's no way."

Well, Maxwell was doing just fine on his own. "What about animal hearts?"

"We eat those too. They can take the edge off, for sure. I know werewolves who have curbed their appetite with animal hearts and attempted to live normal, boring lives. It doesn't work out in the end, but it's a valiant effort."

That's what I had to do then. If Maxwell killed Rich and became human, I would have to learn to shove animal hearts down my throat. Hopefully, that would be enough, and I could still go to family Christmas without wanting to kill my parents.

"Are you really that torn up at the thought of killing a defenseless human?" she asked mockingly.

"Yes!" I didn't understand how no one else could be freaking out about that.

She rolled her eyes. "Humans aren't defenseless. They're animals. They fight, they screw, they kill."

I shook my head. I mean, I guess she was right, but that's not the world I saw when I looked at humanity. "They love, they build families and futures—"

She grabbed my arm and stared into my eyes intensely. "When you mate with your true partner, you'll be connected with him on a level deeper than anything you've ever experienced before. There will be no one else—ever."

I didn't mean to swoon, but it did sound terribly romantic. "Like a penguin?"

The look she gave me was hard to describe, but I knew she thought I was childish. I couldn't help being a little bit of a hopeless romantic. I only had fantasies to believe in. I had never gotten my heart broken before. When I read that a male penguin searches the beach for the perfect stone to present to his lady of choice as a proposal, I died on the inside (in a good way, of course). After they lay their eggs, the couple just sing together for hours. The female leaves for the winter, so she can store up food for her family, and the man protects their chick during the harsh season. When winter is over, they use their song to find each other again, and the momma feeds her baby. As long as they can find each other, they stay together. It was beyond romantic, and it was pure nature.

"If that means it's for forever." Cassandra was obviously annoyed with my naivety. "Look at human divorce rates, compared to our mating rituals, and tell me who has love figured out."

Well, that was hardly fair. I didn't know much about werewolves. I did know about penguins, though. They didn't tend to stray away from their mates. This was true about other animals. Swans, bald eagles, wolves…

"Human brutality is no different than us. We were them. We just evolved."

"Evolution, huh?" Yeah, I found that hard to believe. If humans were gonna evolve, it wouldn't be into heart-eating monsters. That just made us more dependent on humans. "It's not a curse?"

"I suppose a fanatic would see it that way."

"A fanatic?" There seemed to be some part of the conversation I was missing, but she shut her mouth and kept walking with me.

There was a locker room for former employees of the mill, complete with showers. It was a pretty nice place to build a psycho army since they had shelter, space, and running water. I became worried that Rich wasn't completely impulsive, and he actually had a plan figured out.

"Take a shower. You'll feel better once you do."

But the shower was sort of a very open space, and anyone could walk in and see me. I didn't have the girls' locker room experience at school, so no one knew what my body looked like. My mom didn't even know, and Cassandra didn't seem to be moving. "I'll feel better once I'm in my college dorm, hanging pictures of my family, and making detailed calendars."

"Yeah, that sounds very boring."

"My life isn't boring. I am very fulfilled." I defended myself so much; it sounded wooden, like it wasn't real.

"Is that why you're ready and willing to jump the bones of the first boy you find?"

I blushed like he was around to hear what she said. "Maxwell is different."

"Because you already knew each other when you were too young to remember?"

"What do you know about my brother's death?"

Cassandra shrugged, but she was so smug that I didn't believe her. "I know there is a prophecy about a boy who could possibly fit your brother's description. The location, the age, and other features may have led a werewolf clan to believe he was that boy."

"What's the prophecy say?"

"That he will unite or conquer—the translation is a little sketchy—all of our tribes. You can see why it would be crucial to have a boy like that in your clan."

I literally felt ill. My parents suffered every day because of some secret werewolf power struggle? They deserved the truth, but

I wouldn't know what to tell them. "Then why would they kill them?"

"What makes you think he's dead?"

I allowed her to put hope in my head for one single millisecond. But after that, I furiously pushed her. "Don't screw with me! The police said with the amount of blood—"

"They didn't find a body, did they?" Her hand firmly gripped my throat, and I remembered I wasn't the queen of that pack. I tried pulling on her arm, but she proved her superior strength by lifting me into the air. "Your brother's and Maxwell's sister's bodies are still missing to this day. You never found that to be sort of strange?"

How did she expect me to answer if I couldn't breathe?

She let me go, and I fell to my feet, coughing and feeling extremely grateful to be alive. "My parents lied about my past. I didn't know how my brother died. I thought he was hit by a car."

She cocked her brow and chuckled at the absurdity. "I find that a little strange too."

I shook my head. I knew my parents. They lied to me and kept a huge secret, but it couldn't have been any bigger than what it was. "They didn't want this tragedy to define me."

"So, they would rather not have you defined at all?"

I growled. I didn't mean to, but I literally growled like a dog and charged her without even thinking. "Don't talk about my parents!"

She grabbed my shoulders, and I didn't even budge her. She only shook because she chuckled. "I like it when you're angry. It's pretty cute."

I growled again, but she threw me on my back, and I hit my head on the tile. It didn't hurt too badly, but I was stunned for a little bit.

She threw salt in my wounds by turning on the water before I had the chance to undress. "You smell. Take care of yourself, or Maxwell is going to mate for life with someone else."

I think I wanted to attack her again, but I did genuinely need a moment, and she left me alone for a while. I took off my clothes and washed with the liquid soap in a dispenser. I would kill for a real shower. Not literally! I just really wanted to feel normal and safe again.

I wondered if I was ever truly safe, though. If there were some kind of prophecy endangering Kevin, was I always gonna get pulled in? And if Kevin got pulled in, what did that have to do with Annie? Was she supposed to help Kevin unite or conquer the werewolf tribes? Were they still alive somehow and living as monsters? And if they had them, what did Cassandra want with Maxwell? I didn't believe she wanted to get Rich's friend back. There was way more to it than that.

I stayed in the shower for like an hour. Cassandra eventually came back and decided my shower was over by turning off the water. I gave her a nasty scowl, but she chuckled and threw some clothes at me.

They were a little…dark for me, I guess. There was a black lacey tank, a short red skirt, and skanky underwear. It was totally not me, and I felt naughty for even touching them. "Whose clothes are these?"

"Does it matter?"

"It does." I didn't wanna steal from someone she had eaten, but I, sure enough, didn't wanna walk around in wet clothes all day. I didn't need Rich commenting on my bra showing through my shirt or something. He was so jealous of Maxwell that I wouldn't be surprised if he tried to steal me for himself. He totally flirted with me, and Cassandra didn't care. I figured she was his fake girlfriend, but she was a pretty terrible fake girlfriend as well.

I did put on the clothes in question. When I was dressed, I checked myself out in a mirror. It was just new clothes, but I felt different. I started to move my fingers to braid my wet hair, but I stopped and ran my fingers through it instead. I did look really cute…I think. But the longer I stared, the more something changed.

"Oh my gosh!" I blinked, and my eyes changed into that weird wolfie color. I covered my mouth in horror, but then I felt my teeth coming in, and my jaw ached. I was embarrassed when I had to wear braces, and nobody even saw me. How was I supposed to live with those big chompers in my mouth? And just like I suspected, the claws coming up through my fingers on top of my human nails did hurt. They even bled a little bit. I was looking at a full-blown monster, so I didn't think it was so awful to genuinely freak out.

"Jesse?" Cassandra came running to check me out. "What's wrong?"

"I'm a monster! I'm a hideous monster!" I began to cry, and I punched the mirror. I cut my hand, but it didn't hurt much, and that disturbed me. I didn't wanna be a freak.

"Sweetheart…" Cassandra grabbed my shoulders and forced me to walk over to the mirror above the next sink. I tried to fight her off in my hysteria, but she was still much stronger than me in her normal state. "Look at yourself."

"I don't want to."

"I said 'look!'"

I slowly looked at the mirror again and sobbed a bit more. If my parents could see me, they'd be afraid. I couldn't take care of sick little children. I would scare the crap out of them. I was scared of myself!

She grabbed my jaw and forced my face to stay steady, so I couldn't fight off my reflection. "Look at those beautiful eyes."

She truly was weird to think I would love those freaky golden eyes, but…I guess they were incredibly unique when compared to every other pair of eyes on the planet, especially my natural brown eyes. The shimmer was quite pretty.

"Now, take a breath and calm down."

That wasn't exactly the easiest thing in the world to ask, but I did think of Maxwell and how we were alone in that bookstore. He told me to count and start over. "Three…two…one…" I closed my eyes and took a deep breath. I could feel my heart beating so strongly in my chest, but it calmed down, and my jaws and fingers ached again as they receded.

"Good girl." She kissed my cheek and held me for a little while. "You're developing nicely. I think you'd make a great queen."

I shook my head like a stubborn child. "I don't wanna be this."

"Is that true?" She wiped what was left of my tears and hugged my waist. "Sweetie, you are much stronger than you've ever been, and now you're a knockout."

"I haven't physically changed." I looked down at my breasts to make sure. I wasn't more appealing just because I was a wolf.

"Everyone will be able to sense it. Humans and werewolves alike will desire to have you. If you wanna be with Maxwell, be careful. Don't let someone else imprint on you."

"Imprint?" I touched the mark on my shoulder. "Like this?"

"No, it's not physical. It's a mystical bond that you form with your mate. Others will be able to sense it, but not more than you. You'll be partners devoted to one another."

I began to blush. Even without being a wolf, I guess I could sort of tell Maxwell wanted to imprint on me. He admitted to his wolf's desire to change me into what he was. Once he saw I was in the midst of transforming, I wondered if he'd even want to kill Rich. "I wouldn't wanna do that unless I loved somebody."

Cassandra laughed at my childish nonsense. "It's better than love. It's an understanding. It's a necessary means of survival and companionship."

I could understand what she meant just fine, but I saw cartoon movies all the time. I didn't mind falling in love with a beast if his heart truly belonged to me. Maybe we could even break the curse. "But we could love each other? That's allowed?"

She laughed again, but I don't think she was trying to be mean. I'd like to think she found my optimism refreshing. "Yes. Love is definitely allowed."

She let me go, and I still stared in the mirror. I did feel different. Maybe I felt a little bit darker, stronger…sexier? I was afraid of a lot of things, but I wanted a change. I had to push through my fears and learn how to deal with the next chapter of my life. "I'm hungry."

"Good." Cassandra locked her arm with mine. "I shall feed you, my dear."

I really hoped she wasn't talking about people, but how my stomach was beginning to rumble, I was nervous I wouldn't care about that much longer…

Chapter Nine

There were some guys outside grilling burgers. I always thought the smell of them was great, but I never touched them. Mom and Dad ate a lot of vegetarian meals to accommodate me, but they still loved to eat meat. It must have been a pain, but they never complained. Now that I think about it, I never thanked them enough for their sacrifices.

"How's our new blood?" asked one of the boys manning the grill. He was a cute kid, probably barely a freshman in high school, but he looked a little bit like Rich, so I wanted to immediately hate him forever.

"She's progressing fine," Cassandra said. "She's hungry. I wanna get some food in her."

"Here's a plate." A boy with a kind face came from behind. I think he was even blushing. "You've gotta keep up your strength. We've got that big turn coming up tomorrow night."

"Yeah…" I wasn't excited about it at all. I wondered if any other wolves were being held against their will. If I could find someone else to help me, maybe we could jump Rich. Just because we all bowed before him didn't mean we couldn't challenge him. That's what wolves did, right? The strongest leads until another alpha emerges.

The burger set on my plate seemed extra juicy. It was shining. I looked at the other burgers around me, and I saw a lot of pinks and reds. "Are these raw?"

"We prefer them on the rare side. How did you like them as a human?"

"I didn't." A part of me was sickened as I stared at the meat, but it did smell very good, and I was genuinely starving. "Here goes nothing." I took a big bite out of it. My dislike of meat came from when I ate a chicken wing. It seemed so obvious that it was a bird's wing, and I thought about its poor little feathers and trying to fly. I couldn't do it. Then, I tried to eat a steak, but I didn't like the feeling of tearing into the meat. It seemed…brutal?

Suddenly, I found myself enjoying the feeling of tearing into something. I liked the fatty grease in my mouth, and it was juicy, tender, and delicious. I was done in a matter of seconds. "May I please have another?"

Cassandra laughed again and patted my new companion on his back. "Take care of her, Stewart. I'm gonna get some things ready."

I got two more burgers and let him escort me to a log to sit. I was a little busy eating like a savage, but I could tell he was beginning to pine after me. He had puppy eyes, and his voice was shaky like he expected me to take my top off, or something extreme. "It's cool you're here."

"Not really." I covered my mouth so he wouldn't see my food chunks. "I don't like this. I don't like being a werewolf."

"Oh, that can't be true!" He didn't seem like all the other guys. He was small compared to Maxwell in height and muscles. He was wearing a pair of glasses, but the frames were missing. He seemed more like a bookworm than a people eater, but I guess it wasn't my place to judge.

"Why would you like being a werewolf?"

"For starters, I'm much stronger than I used to be. I'm not gonna get thrown into lockers anymore. I'm strong enough to make a difference in the world. I'm like a superhero now!"

"A superhero?" I didn't mean to laugh and snort, but that was rich! "I don't know if you know this, but werewolves eat people. Rich killed Maxwell's mom and his own parents."

"Well, not all of us are like that. We weren't all okay with that, but he's our alpha."

He was gonna be stuck as a werewolf, one way or another, but if it were possible to make him an ally against Rich, I needed to take a shot. "And you haven't hurt anyone?"

"No. I've only been eating normal food and animal hearts. We have a cooler of a bunch of stuff."

"Really?" My stomach still rumbled. It wasn't as bad, but I was craving something other than burgers. I couldn't imagine Maxwell going about an entire month without giving in to temptation a little bit. "Do you know Maxwell?"

"No. I didn't know any of these guys before." All the other guys seemed sort of like athletes. If they weren't built like football players, maybe skater boys. The girls sort of ranged from weird to fabulous. "Rich was going to eat my heart, but I fought him off. He was impressed with the fight in me, so he let me live, and the transformation took over."

Stewart sort of seemed wimpy, but if he put up a good fight while human, maybe he could do something against Rich now. "And you feel fine with him being your alpha?"

"He's not the nicest guy in the world, but we have to belong to a pack. Who else is gonna challenge him?"

I sighed. I barely tried any backstabbing, and I was already exhausted. I had no idea how to take over. The most devious thing I had ever done was to steal Annie's chalk...allegedly. "I just wanna be normal."

"You clearly haven't explored all of the cool things you can do now." He took off his glasses and put them in my hand. "I popped out my lenses because my sight is off the charts."

It was obvious he did that, but I didn't know why. I was freaking out so much about being a werewolf that I didn't take time to notice the world was different. I mean, there was a firefly dancing across the field, and I could follow it when it went out to the tree line when it was dim. I could see the shine on its glossy wings. Its beady little eyes were disgusting, and its long body just reminded me of a huge larva. I don't know why that's the first thing I decided to take notice of, but I was grossed out. "I guess you're right. My vision is better."

"And your smell. Tell me you can't smell what I ate three days ago." He practically shoved his face into my nostrils!

"Gross!" I pushed him a little too hard, and he flew right off the log. I don't think he ate anything other than meat. There was definitely bourbon. I knew the smell from my dad. He wasn't drunk. He must have had it yesterday.

"Seriously, though." Stewart brushed the dirt off himself and laughed. "All of our senses are heightened. I'm told sex is like a hundred percent increase."

"You've been told?"

"I mean..." He turned bright red like a tomato. "I haven't exactly done it before."

"Okay…" I was blushing then, but it's not because it was a cute moment. I was nervous about what Cassandra said. I didn't wanna attract an army of wolf boys. "I think I'm gonna go now."

"I'm sorry." Stewart ran in front of me before I could walk away. "I didn't mean to upset you or anything. You're just really pretty, I know most of us are kind of paired up, and—"

"If you think we're called to some higher purpose, it's not so you can lose your virginity to me in a frisky, supernatural way. We're cursed because a little boy is playing king, and I'm not a part of this nonsense." I pushed him out of my way and stormed off. I could feel my heart racing again. I was so angry, and I didn't understand how fierce I was until I stopped a good twenty feet away from him.

Cassandra loomed onto the scene, out of nowhere, smiling. "You're certainly getting tough. Are you going to challenge Rich for alpha?"

I stopped and turned to her. "Can a female wolf do that? Can she lead a pack?"

"The strongest leads. We're not sexist." I had no idea what she was trying to pull, but maybe she would come right out and say it eventually. She couldn't be asking me to take down Rich. That would be absurd.

I wasn't acting or feeling like myself. I never pushed people or raised my voice. If Rich found out what I said about him, I'd probably be dead. "Maybe I should go lock myself back up in the water tower—"

"Come on." She grabbed my hand and ran with me. "I wanna show you something."

There were a couple of cars, and she led me to mine, which they apparently stole. At least my stuff was still there, but they totally went through it. My boxes were not in the positions I left them in. And if she had my clothes the entire time, why didn't she just give those to me instead of making me look like some hoochie? "Where are we going?"

She winked and got on the driver's side. "Somewhere we can have some fun."

I threw my head back and growled. I was so not cool with going out with a mastermind werewolf, but it was odd how I ended up listening to everything she told me to do. Maybe it was because I was a little afraid, or because she had information I needed. The hold she had on me was troubling. "Why are you so interested in me?"

"You're our newest recruit."

"Did you usher in Stewart?"

She grinned hard. "I show attention to all of my wolves."

"Your wolves? I thought this was Rich's pack."

"Only because I turned him. I have no interest in running this pack. I only wanted to make it and guide my successor. This isn't my first rodeo." She was strange, beautiful, cunning, and very dangerous. I really hated her, but for some strange reason, I honestly wanted to be like her. I didn't really want the whole killer demon wolf thing, but her confidence was nice.

"Where do you come from? Are you like the queen of werewolves?"

"I'm not some kind of original werewolf if that's what you're asking. I had a maker, and my maker was made, and so on."

"I know if Maxwell or I kill Rich before the full moon, we'll go back to normal. What would happen if someone killed you?"

"It won't save you." I didn't know if I should believe her, but she was so smug that I was inclined to. "Only you or Maxwell can be saved, and that's only if one of you can kill Rich before the full moon."

"Rich thinks you're his girlfriend."

"We've messed around, sure, but he knows he could never imprint on me. He's too weak."

"So, what are you trying to do? You're not looking for love or companionship."

"I want my pack to be strong. That's all. Rich will have to prove himself, just like all the other alphas in every other pack. If he can kill Maxwell, then I'll know if he's worthy." She turned to me and grinned. "You'll all know."

Could it really be that simple? She thought Maxwell would be a good challenge for Rich? There had to be more. She was far too intrigued by the fact that we both knew each other from long ago. Sooner or later, I would make her reveal the truth to me.

I was horrified when she pulled up to a bar. Cassandra was so excited. She clapped and swayed her head as soon as she took my keys from the ignition. She didn't care about my bulging eyes or hanging mouth. "I'm so underage!"

"You don't have to drink!" Cassandra slapped my leg playfully. "I don't wanna see what a drunk and hungry werewolf can do anyway. All of these humans would probably be dead by the morning."

Humans. People. I hadn't been around any since my transformation, and my crazy werewolf smell was beginning to kick in. I could smell the bad cologne and body spray. I could smell the beer, bourbon, and whiskey. Someone was super musty. But even with all those things going on, they still smelled...delicious. "I can't go in there."

"You have to trust yourself, Jesse. Do you think Maxwell can ever trust you if you can't demonstrate the tiniest bit of restraint against these humans?"

I would feel like such a total failure if I couldn't hold out a little while. If I couldn't handle a couple of strangers, how was I supposed to go to school every day and deal with cheerleaders and mean professors? "Fine."

It was loud, and it got way louder when the doors opened. The music was screaming at me. I almost ran back to the car, but Cassandra grabbed my arm and pulled me through.

We didn't get stopped. I guess we both looked like we could have been the proper drinking age, but we certainly looked a whole lot younger than most of the guys in there. Some middle-aged women were bleeding our ears with their terrible singing on stage. My ears were fine-tuned from years of playing the flute, but this was a special sort of torture I endured. I guess wolf ears made everything crazier.

"Do you like karaoke?"

I was terrified to answer. "Sometimes, I'll sing with my parents..." I certainly didn't wanna perform in front of a bunch of grungy strangers.

Cassandra couldn't take a hint, and she pulled me to the stage as soon as the women were done ripping my ears to shreds. "I'm gonna assume you don't know any current pop ballads then, huh?"

I was nervous while watching the crowd. They did not look happy about us singing, and after the last duet, I couldn't blame them. But even with their scowls, my heart raced, and hunger tripled. I held my rumbling stomach and grunted as it attacked me. I didn't understand how Cassandra could be free from it.

"Yo, what genre?"

"Rock or country. My dad is a big rock fan." I held my head and closed my eyes. I could tell each person apart by their different smells, but they were all blending. They were a herd of cattle, and I didn't feel like a person anymore. I didn't know what I was or what I felt, besides the ravenous hunger.

"Lighten up." Cassandra pressed her back to me and flipped her hair when the music started. She couldn't really sing that well herself, but it was clear from the first hip roll that she was planning on playing off her sex appeal. The crowd was starting to go crazy with it, even though I was uncomfortable.

I had a pretty decent voice, but I never sang in front of a crowd. I was more like a background vocalist, I think. I wasn't meant to perform and have strange men stare at me like a piece of meat. It was ironic that they looked at me and emoted the way I felt about them.

Cassandra wouldn't let me be dull. She grabbed my hips and made me rock them back and forth. The crowd really started howling at that point. I stepped away from her and shook a little bit on my own, but she certainly didn't have to touch me.

Cassandra didn't need a buddy to be out of control. The way she danced made me blush. I had to look away, but it was such a crazy performance that I had to see it. It was sort of like a traffic accident. She even jumped off the stage and jumped on the bar. I can't believe the bartender didn't tackle her. He was too busy looking at her butt.

I was trapped in a bad teen movie that my parents would never let me watch. I told my parents I wouldn't explore my sexuality, talk to strangers, or do anything other than drive straight to college. How could I end up in a bar singing with a frisky werewolf while I struggled with my desire to eat all the people?

I just tried to keep singing, but my stomach was doing cartwheels. One guy was admiring me instead of watching Cassandra make a parody out of us. I think he was healthier compared to a lot of the other people in the bar. He didn't smell too boozy, and I smelled broccoli and roasted carrots as he breathed in and out—slowly—while I hypnotized him with my less-than-ideal hips. I bet he was going to taste yummy.

I shook my head and fought off the idea. It was totally sick of me to think that, but my hunger didn't subside. Suddenly, he was the only smell in the room. He was in my nose and my lungs. I closed my eyes, so I wouldn't have to look at him, but then the rest of the world got a whole lot quieter, and the deep booming of his heart was the lead soloist in the choir of my insanity.

I could feel myself changing. My gums were sore, and I don't know how to even describe what my eyes felt like. I ran off the stage and outside to my car. I was totally wolfing out, but I wasn't so afraid of my reflection anymore. I was just afraid of what I might do if I couldn't get that man's "meat stewing in red wine and vegetables" scent out of my nose.

"What would Maxwell do? What would Maxwell do?" I took a deep breath to calm myself. It slowed my heart, but it didn't help with the smell. If anything, I made it worse. I could practically taste that smell. It was so irritating! But if Maxwell could fight off the intense feeling to eat and or bite me, I had to find that strength too. I was capable. I had to be!

I closed my eyes and took a couple of seconds to focus. I could feel my super fangs receding, which is something I never thought would stop feeling weird. The smell was still there, and it was strong, but I was going to manage. There were other nasty smells to focus on. I was right near a dumpster. If I focused on the awful smell of rotting chicken fat, I would be cool.

"You were great out there."

I grumbled to myself and threw my head back. I was sincerely trying not to kill him, and he wasn't helping me at all. "You should really not be here…"

"But I was curious about you. When I saw you jump on stage, I had to meet you."

I slowly turned around—in case he was a pervert intending on pinning me down—but I stepped closer to my car. "You really shouldn't follow strange women out of bars. You never know what they're like, and that shows poor judgment on your part."

"I'm sorry. You're just so beautiful…" He wasn't that bad-looking himself. He was a bit rugged, but not as rugged as Maxwell. Compared to Maxwell, he could have built teddy bears for a living. The thing that set him apart from the crowded bar was that delicious smell…

"You should really not be around me. I want you to go." I pulled on the handle of my car door. It was messed up that I couldn't open it, but Cassandra still had the keys.

"I will, I just…" He didn't look okay. I think I might have been corrupting him with my wolfiness. His eyes were real whacked out.

My jaws ached again, and my stomach was throbbing. I turned to the car and grabbed the frame. I grunted and squeezed my fingers on the roof, and I gasped when I heard it buckle. "Crap! That's leased!"

"You're gorgeous," his voice quivered. "Do you think we could get a drink together?"

I was surprised at my sudden strength, but that was eclipsed by the sound of his heart pumping in my ears, his yummy smell filling up my nostrils, and I didn't even remember who I was anymore. When he touched my shoulder, I tossed him up against the car and growled like a genuine monster.

I remembered the fear in his eyes. It was the liveliest expression I had ever seen—a glittering light that never wanted to be extinguished. He truly wanted to live so badly, but honestly, I just wanted to eat him!

I scratched his chest, and his blood splattered on me. The smell of it excited me, but there was enough of me left that was startled by it. I never liked blood before my transformation, but I adored it now. I remembered it being everywhere, and the rusty scent was in my nostrils.

My hand grasped his mouth firmly. I had regained enough of myself to know that him screaming for his life, while I was covered in his blood, reflected very poorly on me. "Please, calm down! I didn't mean it." But I really did, and now it was terrible how much I wanted to eat him. There was blood on my fingers, and I was curious how it would taste. I had sucked blood from a cut finger before, but this was so intense. I wasn't even sure I was a werewolf anymore. Maybe I was a vampire!

"You have to kill him," Cassandra said nonchalantly from behind. "You have to kill him, and we have to dump the body before it's too late."

My body was in full-wolf mode. I could feel it, and there was incredible strength in my hands. I thought I was going to break his jaw. It was as if the moon lit my blood on fire. I couldn't imagine how crazy I would feel tomorrow when the moon was about to rise. "I can't…"

"It's simple. Shove your fist straight through his heart and put it in a doggy bag to go. I'll help you put his body in the car."

I closed my eyes and gritted my fangs together as I shoved my hunger deep inside of me. I had to remember I was a human, and my parents would be mortified with what I was becoming. I had to stop it somehow. "I won't do it."

Cassandra threw her head back and groaned. "You're such a coward."

I screamed when her swift fingers slashed across his neck. Then, blood flooded from the open slit and down his chest. I let him go, and his body fell to the ground. He was still, and the color from his face was already gone.

I took a deep breath and stared at him for a little while. I knew he wasn't getting back up, but I really needed him to. I mean, it was my fault he was dead. My wolfiness lured him in, and I attacked him like an animal. "What have I done?"

"Practically nothing, and that's why you're weak."

I snapped my head at her. I was so furious; I thought I would jump right on her, but I lost my nerve somewhere in the middle of my head turn. I think it was when I caught a glimpse of the same blood on her hands that were also on mine.

I don't know why I didn't wrestle her to take my car back, but I made a run for it. I had no idea where I was going, where I'd end up, or what I was trying to accomplish, but I needed to get away from the smell of the blood. I couldn't allow myself to go back and taste the heart of the man who was dead because of me.

Chapter Ten

My sense of direction must have been remarkably wonderful or horribly ridiculous. I kept running and running until I headed straight back to the camp. I didn't think I was paying attention to how to get back when we left, and even if I were, the human me would have never been able to remember anyway.

There was a group of wolves standing by a campfire, and my stomach danced at the thought of food. The sucky thing about it was that I wasn't craving people food. Eating a juicy hamburger might have temporarily ended my hunger, but I had the horrible feeling it wouldn't be enough. Maxwell wouldn't have eaten a dog if it weren't necessary.

I saw Stewart watching me from a distance. He was sitting off to the side with a tough-looking girl with short hair. I rubbed my rumbling stomach and walked over to him with my head hanging low. I didn't want to eat an animal, but it would have been better than eating a person.

I caught Cassandra sitting by the campfire with Rich. I saw her smile, and I wanted to lunge at her. I could smell the man she killed as she breathed. I think Rich had some of him too. That poor man's scent was everywhere around me. I wish I had collapsed from guilt, but my hunger was driving me.

"Hey, Stewart."

"Hey, Jesse." He stood up and smiled like the other girl didn't exist. I guess they weren't a couple. "What's up?"

"She's hungry," the girl said teasingly. "I can see it in her face."

I didn't know I was making a "hungry" expression. It made me self-conscious. "She's amazingly right. I'm starving. I almost killed somebody."

"Why didn't you?" the girl asked.

"Don't mind Kendell. She sort of embraced her role."

I didn't know if she was one of the wolves who attacked Maxwell's family, but she seemed smug. I didn't get the feeling she was vicious, though. I believed she would kill, but I wasn't intimidated.

I think the only wolves who intimidated me were Cassandra and Rich, but Cassandra definitely inched him out.

"Can you help me, Stewart? Do we have any animals I can maybe...?" I threw my head back and sighed. I didn't even want to admit it, but I wouldn't be able to sleep or think with my stomach caving in on itself, and my head was starting to pulse. "Do you have any animal hearts I could try out?"

"Of course. We keep a fridge full."

"Really?" I was surprised I was so happy about that. "Can I have one?"

Stewart laughed a little and signaled me to follow him.

I went back to the abandoned factory with him. There was a big commercial kitchen in there. It was clean, but I could smell the rusty scent of blood, and it only made the hunger pound in my head until my ears shook. I don't even think I could see straight. "And you're sure it's animal hearts?"

"Yeah." He opened a refrigerator, and I saw a diverse library of different hearts in plastic bags. I observed them for myself to make sure. There were small ones that must have belonged to chickens. I didn't get to do a pig dissection since I was homeschooled, but I watched a video about it. The pig heart seemed shorter and maybe a little bit rounder, but I honestly wasn't positive in my state of mind. Then, I saw something a little bigger labeled as buffalo.

"Whatcha thinking?"

As I held it in my hands, I took in the scent of it. There was still blood on it. It was fresh, and I lost myself as the aroma came into my nose. It was probably a great alternative. "And you're sure this is buffalo?"

"I've been eating it since I got here."

Every nerve was telling me to take a bite of it. My teeth enlarged, and my nails were beginning to grow out. My eyes probably changed as well. "And it's buffalo?"

"I'm sure. We need to consume hearts. It doesn't have to be human hearts. If you don't, you'll never get control, and you'll probably end up hurting somebody."

That was enough of a push to give it a try. It was just a dead animal's heart. I took it out of the plastic bag and looked at it for a little while. I imagined myself ripping it out of that man's body and watching it still beat in my hand. Is it sick that I still wanted to eat it? Stupid question. It was even worse when I pressed my tongue to it, just for a quick taste. Once my tongue soaked in that salty yet sweet goodness, I felt the monster in me come out.

It was tough but easy to chew through with my nasty wolf teeth. The outside texture of it reminded me of a liver, but it also sort of had a pâté thing going on, too. It's hard to describe something like a raw heart. It certainly didn't taste like chicken. It didn't really taste like beef either. But whatever it was, it was my new favorite thing.

"What's happening to me?" About halfway through my devouring, I dropped to my knees and moaned in wicked pleasure. I could feel myself changing ever since I was bitten, but for the first time, I felt something else poking at me from the inside. Then, it suddenly became a jab. "Stewart, help me!"

"You're fine. You're just becoming more of yourself."

"Of myself?" I didn't feel like what I used to be. I wanted to be afraid, but I honestly felt stronger than ever. The blood flowing through my veins felt like fire, but there was an ease on my skin, like the way Maxwell would've made me feel if we could touch. It was wild and intense. But the part that made me feel a little uneasy was how my senses seemed to rapidly increase. I could smell more victims to devour. "This isn't me."

"Being a werewolf isn't just about the scary stuff." Stewart pulled on my arm, and I rose to my feet.

"It's not?"

"No. Totally not. I used to get picked on all the time, but now I'm strong, and I'm fast. I'm one of the toughest wolves here."

"Really?" I didn't mean to cock my brow. I just felt like he was challenging me, and I didn't like that he might have thought he could win. Maybe it was a wolfie thing.

"Run with me."

"I just ran from that town all the way here. I think I've done enough running!"

"Okay." He said that, but I knew by the mischievous look in his eye that he wasn't going to stop. I should have counted to three because he quickly changed his mind and shoved my arm. "Tag!"

He took off running, but I was determined not to run after that immature boy. I never had to play tag with anyone. There were no kids around me growing up, but I did feel like I should run after him. It was a crazy and strong urge that had my feet moving before I could even stop myself.

Stewart looked like a little boy, but he was quick, and he could jump. His nimble feet jumped wall to wall, and he leaped onto the balcony. I didn't feel nearly that confident, but I didn't want to lose him. I jumped for the wall and, surprisingly, started scaling it. I looked down below once I got up on the balcony. It was at least three stories high. "Wow..."

Stewart ran out of my line of sight, but I could smell him. He smelled like fruity liquor, cheese, meat, and campfire smoke. I also heard his feet pounding on the tiled floors of the factory.

I laughed short and very amazed. I was incredibly capable of tracking Stewart, and I could totally put him down if I wanted to. I could feel the wolfie part of me becoming excited about proving my superiority. It was thrilling because I had already seen the outcome. That made me not afraid to just punch it!

I took off running with my nose as my guide. Stewart ran into an office and jumped right out of the window. I sniffed for good measure, but I could smell that he slid down a ladder and onto the grass. I could see him heading for the tree line, and I smiled.

I knew climbing down was a waste of time, so I didn't. I took a few steps back, jumped off the building, and landed right on my feet. I felt like I was watching an action hero play out a movie in my body.

I heard cheers from the rest of the wolves engaged in the race, and I heard most of them saying my name. I didn't know what I had done to gain their support, but it was awesome to feel like I was a part of a team.

I didn't realize I was close to catching Stewart until his eyes bucked. He made things more complicated when we got into the woods. He jumped from tree to tree like they were steps. I didn't do the whole parkour thing, but I had a feeling I could. I concentrated on moving my feet. I had already come so far. I could win!

Stewart became more panicked, and instead of taking my tackle like a man, he grabbed onto a tree and ran up it like a squirrel. I paused for a second. He was going up pretty high. Then, he jumped through the trees. Maybe he was part monkey, but I sure wasn't.

"Did he seriously climb up the tree?" Rich asked from behind. "I hate when he does that."

I didn't wanna talk to Rich, but I was curious. "Why is he so good at that?"

"Some of us are more talented than others. When he transformed, he became incredible. He's one of my best." He looked at me and smirked. "I would say you fit into that category."

Oh, geez. I really hoped he didn't honestly like me. He did bite and turn me into a monster. "You think you've given me some kind of gift?"

"Haven't I?" He pointed to all the other members of our pack that came into the trees. They wanted to see if I would manage the impossible and catch their little spider monkey. They were strong, they were unified, and they seemed to be at peace with what they were. I felt them daring me to disagree with them.

"Do you not feel like a better you?" Cassandra asked.

"You killed that man—"

"That's not what she asked you," Rich annoyingly pointed out. "Don't you feel more impressive than you ever have?"

Physically, that was a given, but I was not okay with hurting people and craving human hearts. How was being a werewolf gonna improve my life when I wanted to be a doctor and save lives? "I just wanna go to college and be normal."

"We're the greatest sorority in the country!" Rich said laughingly. "Don't defect from us now."

I felt a little threatened. What would happen to a wolf if they didn't have protection from their pack? What would happen if I stood against them all? I knew what they did to Maxwell's family. I had to protect my parents. "I guess I'm not defecting…"

"Good." He stroked my cheek like a creeper. "Then run with us."

"Run with you?"

Stewart jumped from the trees and landed on his feet. He was such a man-cat. "It'll be awesome. Aren't you having fun?"

"Yeah, aren't you having fun?" One of the other wolves mocked poor Stewart. The crowd laughed, but Stewart didn't care. He was a true contender when it came to them.

"I guess I'm having a little bit of fun." I was trying new things. I was capable of so much more now. I was horrified about what I was becoming, but I couldn't lie about the excitement. "I think I would like to continue running."

"Good." Rich decided to be way over the top and took off his shirt. Lots of other boys did the same, including petite Stewart. He was a bit gangly, but he did have abs and nice biceps on his little arms. Maybe they were trying to entice me, but I wasn't feeling it. If I wanted to think of someone hunky, I would think of my dear Maxwell.

I wondered what Maxwell was doing. He should have been chasing me down. He must have been close. He wouldn't abandon me, but I wondered what would happen when he did. I couldn't let him sacrifice his humanity for me. Maybe…just maybe I could get used to being a monster. The worst thing would be for the two of us to be trapped in the nightmare together.

Rich smiled and tilted his head to the side, and that made him look a bit more attractive to my eyes. "Follow me." He was charming. He was bold. He was ambitious. I could see why all the wolves stayed in line and followed him through the woods. I ran with them, too, but it wasn't because of Rich. I ran because I needed to understand something about myself. I needed to know if I could feel what they felt. I needed to know if the animal instinct was something invading me, or if it always wanted to come out. I was certain, from the time I was bitten, of my answer. Now, things were unclear. I had to continue running to feel the earth beneath my feet, and the honest rhythm of my rapid-fire heart. The more I ran, the more I could know myself.

Chapter Eleven

I wasn't used to being around many people—especially members of the opposite sex—so it was strange waking up with my head against a boy's shoulder. His name was Robbie, and it didn't mean anything. His girlfriend was on his other shoulder, and Stewart was resting on my stomach. We ran for a long time, most of them got wasted, and I watched. I knew while I watched them, I was being assessed.

"Did you have a nice night?" Rich asked.

I sat up, and Stewart reluctantly rolled off me. I couldn't believe I had fallen asleep next to a roaring campfire, but it was very nice. My parents' idea of camping was setting up a fort in my bedroom. My stars were glowing constellation stickers. My campfire was an overheated flashlight that warmed my toes when it got too close.

The entire pack slept outside together. Rich was directly across from me. He watched me practically the entire night, even though I was a wallflower the whole time. Cassandra tried to pull me off my feet for a dance, but I fought her every time. She would get bored and dance with Rich, and most of it was dirty music video stuff. I really tried not to watch, but this was an all-night party. The weirdest thing about it was that Cassandra knew Rich was watching me, and she seemed to get off on the fact that he wanted me. Did they think they were enticing me? If they did, they were wrong.

They convinced me I was stronger. They did convince me I was more attractive than I had ever felt before. But the one thing they were never going to convince me of was being a proper queen for Rich. I would never fall for his flirty eyes and smug smirks. Besides the fact that I wanted him dead, so either Maxwell or I could live normally, I could sense he wasn't up to par. I couldn't let him tame me. He wasn't strong enough.

"Are you hungry?" Stewart asked.

"I am, but I wanna shower first." I got some of my clothes from the car and went into the mill. There were eight girls—nine, including me—and they were all close. They were all obsessed with Cassandra. She was how I imagined the popular girl in high school to be. All the boys wanted to be with her, and all the girls wanted to be her. Even I had a strange fascination with her.

I tried not to look at her in the shower. It seemed rude, and I didn't want Cassandra to think I was into her or anything, but I was curious. She was voluptuous, but not big at all. She was exotic, and she stood out in a very good way. Everyone considered her to be one of our own, but her tribal mark was different than ours. It was similar but maybe a little more advanced. I wondered how far up the food chain she might have been. However far it was, I had a sense that I didn't wanna screw around with her.

After I got dressed, I followed the girls into the dining hall. One of the girls was younger than all of us. She must have been thirteen, but she was at our wild party last night. I did see Rich get a little feisty with her when she tried to take some booze. "Are you Rich's little sister?"

"Yeah, I'm Rachel." She had shoulder-length black hair and bright blue eyes. She looked as sweet as apple pie, honestly.

"Rachel?" I tried to sound friendly, but I was plotting to kill her brother. It was a little unsettling. "I guess it's nice for Rich to have his little sister and brother here with him."

"It's weird being in his pack, though. He's my big brother, so I knew he was always gonna boss me around forever, but this is different."

"Do you like it? I mean…" I took a deep breath. "I did hear what happened to your parents and—"

"My parents wouldn't listen." She laughed, and it gave me the creeps. "Rich did what he had to do for my brother and me. We were never gonna amount to anything while being the children of crappy mechanics. They didn't even leave us with two dimes to rub together."

"Yeah, but did they love you?"

"In their own human way, I guess they did. We loved them too, but they didn't wanna evolve, and we did."

I so did not know what I should say to the little psychopath. I sort of felt like I should slap her and call her an ungrateful brat for abandoning her parents. "I would never just decide that my parents weren't worth anything to me."

"Then why are you here instead of at home with them?"

"Because I was on my way to college before Cassandra kidnapped me, and Rich bit me!" I might have been incredibly timid before, but I wasn't going to let a child confuse me for one of them. I was not evil, crazy, or unfaithful to my parents.

"You could leave the pack, but there are always consequences when you do." That little girl stepped right up to my face, and she smiled like the devil. "The choice is yours."

I was not intimidated, but I just did not know what to do. The rest of the girls were watching. Should I have hit her? Should I have rammed her against a wall to prove my authority? Should I have wept for the death of her humanity? I just didn't know.

She smirked at me and walked away. The other girls followed Rachel to breakfast. Cassandra stayed behind with me to laugh at my shock and awe. "She's a bloodhound. It's always the youngest who turns out to be the craziest, especially if they're quiet."

"And what's her role in all of this? What happens if her brother gets knocked down by Maxwell—?"

"Or you?"

I laughed it off. "I'm not challenging Rich for leadership of the pack. I wouldn't take the opportunity for humanity away from Maxwell."

"And you—like young Rachel—have evolved."

"Not by choice!"

"Evolution never happens out of choice. Evolution happens out of necessity." She lightly punched my chin and rushed off to the dining hall.

I dragged my feet. The boys were nice and prepared breakfast. I could smell the steak and eggs as soon as I got out of the shower. Everyone was joking around and laughing. The youngest boy grabbed an apple from Stewart's tray and made a run for it. He didn't get too far. I recognized the boy was Rich's younger brother, Dennis. He was too young to be involved with a pack of killers, but they were naïve and easily swayed.

Rich had Cassandra on one side of him, but there was an empty chair reserved for me. I sort of wanted to sit with Stewart, but with the full moon so close, I didn't want to rock the boat.

I took my place and ate my food. Rich didn't say anything for a long time, but he watched and smiled. I was starving, so I scarfed down my food as dignified as I could. I would have to apologize to Maxwell if I ever looked at him like he was a freak.

I found it hard to believe Rich wasn't hungry, but he didn't even touch his plate. He leaned over the table and got as close to the front of my face as possible. "Are you excited?"

"About what?"

"The full moon tonight." He was giddy, like how I would be the night before Christmas.

"Why would I be excited about my humanity ending?"

"You can barely say that with a straight face!"

I could feel a small smile on my lips. I didn't mean to be comfortable with the pack, but I did at least a little bit. I didn't feel like I was figuring myself out when I woke up in the morning. I didn't have any questions. "You know Maxwell will come for me."

"If he gets past some of my boys." He had a forkful of eggs and smiled widely.

I glanced around the room and realized some of the boys were missing. There were usually thirteen altogether, and now, there were eleven. "You sent some of our pack after Maxwell?"

"I did."

Cassandra was smiling, but she didn't seem happy about it. She wanted Rich to be challenged, but he was just too naïve to see it.

I didn't want Maxwell to get hurt. One wolf was gonna be hard enough. I didn't think he'd have to challenge an army. "Are you scared of him?"

He laughed—not forcibly either—but he was also very offended. "You're asking me if I'm afraid of a man who literally can't touch people. He poses absolutely no threat to me."

"Then why won't you face him like a man?" I didn't mean to scream it out, but everyone certainly heard, and they all stared at us.

Cassandra wasn't helping with Rich's mindset. She was about to laugh at the various shades of red on his face. She had to turn her head away.

Rich got even closer—nose to nose—and he seethed his words. "If Maxwell can fight past two of my men, he can come and challenge me. If he doesn't, then he was never worthy to lead this pack."

"This is my brother's pack," Rachel interjected. The middle brother shushed her and held her face.

I was between feeling the wrath of my alpha and fighting the courage to overtake him. I think I did want to fight him, but I wasn't one hundred percent certain if I was going to win. Maxwell? I knew he would, without a shadow of a doubt. "Give him a chance…"

"I'm sorry," he shouted. "I can't hear you all too well. Speak up."

I think he expected me to flinch or back down, but I was ready for a fight. Maybe it was the moon, but I was feeling kind of hardcore. "Maxwell deserves a fair chance."

"Everyone here falls under my pack. They would all go to war for me, including you. If that's untrue, let me know. You can challenge me for leadership. After I beat you into submission, if you still refuse, I will snap your neck and send your ashes to your parents!"

There was a rush in my chest and electricity surging through my veins. I honestly wanted to fight. I was being backed into a corner, and I wanted to wildly swing to break free. But I wasn't an animal. I was still a naïve young woman who believed in those silly girly movies about a prince coming to save me.

But if Maxwell really didn't show up to fight Rich and reclaim his humanity, I was going to claw his throat out.

"Calm down, Richard." Cassandra pushed on Rich's chest to get him away from me. "You know this little wolf is one of us. She's totally sold. Don't be dramatic."

But I had struck a nerve, and he wouldn't stop glaring. The more he glared, the more ferocious his eyes became. "Get her out of my sight."

No one was going to defend me in that room. The only one who felt like they could publicly go against him was Cassandra, and she was too smart to do that. "Come on, Jesse. We have to get rid of some of this aggression."

As she pulled me away by my arm, my eyes had changed as well. I was legitimately close to lunging at Rich and tearing him apart! "What's the matter with me?"

"Well, the full moon is almost upon us, and I know you feel like you're bursting out of your skin."

I rubbed my hands. My claws were ready to pop right out. "I feel no such thing."

"Don't be embarrassed," she laughed. "It's perfectly natural for you to get riled up, in more ways than one." I didn't exactly know what she was talking about, but she was being dirty. "Why don't you try releasing some of that tension by fighting me?"

"What?" I laughed short. "No!"

"Why not?" She was so totally serious.

I looked around the facility to see if anyone was following us. We were on our way out of the building, and I guess they were all busy eating. That was good. I didn't want them to see me get my butt whipped. "I'm not gonna win, am I?"

She cocked her brow. "You can sense that?" I think she was honestly impressed.

"I guess." I didn't feel too ashamed about it. This may sound stupid, but I was a little flattered that she even wanted to fight me. "You're not a normal werewolf. There's something weird about your mark."

"I'm high up in the ranks. How far? I won't say."

"Why are you debasing yourself with Rich?"

She got a good laugh out of that. "I told you I look out for my own. I build packs and let them become strong. I've been doing this for a long time."

"Are you immortal or something?"

"No. No creature is truly immortal. Ageless? I'm afraid we're not that either, but we retain our youth longer than an average human."

I looked around. They had a good thing going with the abandoned mill, but I didn't know how covert they were or how chaotic things would be after they all transformed. But I had to assume Cassandra knew what she was doing. "So, this is truly just to build a legacy or a strong pack?"

"What did you think it was?"

I was so embarrassed; I turned as red as a cherry tomato. "I was concerned you were making a pack and trying to hook up with a strong leader. I figured you were trying to get rid of Rich, so Maxwell could be a more suitable mate, or something crazy." I wished we were on a beach, so I could bury myself in the sand or drown in the water.

"No!" She laughed and patted my back. "I see you're sprung for him. Besides, I am deeply involved with someone else."

I did a double-take. "Then why are you messing around with Rich?" I didn't get infidelity. I figured it was for the insanely screwed up, but Cassandra didn't seem crazy. She was strategic.

"Things are complicated between my friend and me. He's not exactly cut from the same cloth as us."

"Is he a human?" I'm not sure why I whispered that, but I did.

She rolled her eyes. "If he were, I'd just sink my teeth into him. It's not that simple."

"Is he from a different pack? Is it forbidden love?"

"That is enough talk about love." She pushed me on my shoulder and nearly knocked me off my heels. "I want to fight."

"Why?"

"Because I'm determined to make you strong! I know you're capable of being a great queen."

It was weird. I was never competitive before, but I did wanna tackle her. I didn't want to lose, but there might have been the slightest chance that I could take her. And even if I lost, I'd get stronger. Wouldn't I? It was crazy, though. "What if I don't wanna be a werewolf?"

"You give me a reason why you don't, and I'll convince you otherwise."

"I don't wanna eat people!" That sort of seemed like the number one reason. I shouldn't have had to bring that up.

"You'll get over it."

My mouth dropped in pure dismay, but I accidentally laughed. "That so does not help your case!"

"Do you really wanna force that much humanity down your throat? Do you wanna think about all of these strangers you don't know?" I found it hard to believe she didn't care about humanity, but I could clearly see it in her eyes. She was a shark—well, no! That was the wrong word. She was a wolf.

I wasn't like that, though. I know I rejected Maxwell when I saw him helpless on the side of the road, but I drove him across the country. I was a good person. "I wanna help people. That's why I wanna be a doctor."

"No, you wanna be a doctor to feel like you matter. All these years, you've been sheltered. You've barely lived in this world at all."

"That's why I decided to go to college on my own. I don't need to be a werewolf to get what I want."

"Maybe not, but I assure you, it's better this way." She was so cool and suave as she circled around me, like the moon orbiting the earth or the earth around the sun. But maybe I was being naïve. Maybe I was orbiting her, even though it felt like I was standing still.

"Better for who? We're a scary epidemic that could potentially end our world. How are my parents supposed to survive in a world like this?"

Her slender yet strong fingers rested on my shoulder, and she spoke in my ear. "Werewolves have been in this world a lot longer than modern medicine. We've remained hidden, but powerful. We want our packs to reign and rule, but we have no immediate plans to take over the humans. We have other wars to wage."

I stepped away from her and turned around. "With who?"

She crossed her arms. Why was she getting such a kick out of feeding me a breadcrumb's worth of information? "Our pack is connected to a clan leader. There are several, and we don't get along with each other. That's why people like your brother are so important, and now, Maxwell."

"Were," I interjected sadly.

"What?"

I nervously laughed, though I was certain she misspoke. "You said 'are' as if he were still a player. If he's still a player, that means he's still alive…"

She cocked her brow and smiled. "Did I?"

I was still very confused. There was nobody, but Maxwell and my parents were pretty sure. And Cassandra made it vaguely clear that her wolves had nothing to do with it. She wasn't there. How would she know if he were alive? Unless she laid eyes on him or something…!

"Don't mess with me!" I became so furious with her that I just lashed out and pushed her. She stumbled back, but she planted her feet into the ground. I think I might have strangled her, but she was strong and fast enough to grab my arms. "Is my brother alive?"

Cassandra was so much stronger than I; she tossed me on the ground like an impatient child bored with her toy. But I guess saying that she was "bored" was completely wrong. She was certainly enjoying every moment of antagonizing me. "If you want the answers, you fight for them."

I couldn't even think about the fact that I would lose against her. I had to know for my parents, and for Maxwell. If Kevin were alive, that meant Annie might have been safe with him somewhere as well. That was worth fighting for, instead of some wolfie instinct.

"Look at you!" she beamed with pride. "Your wolf side is coming out."

I could feel the change coming over me. My jaw and fingers hurt, but I was too angry to care. I didn't like not feeling in control of my emotions, but there was also a thrill I couldn't deny. I was starting to realize why Maxwell thought he could overcome his haphephobia long enough to kill Rich.

I, quite literally, growled and charged at her. Cassandra still looked normal, so I thought I would have the upper hand. When she easily tossed me on my back, I knew I was mistaken. I did wonder how strong she would have been while transformed, but I certainly didn't stop. I couldn't stop until she told me the truth.

I tried clawing her face off, but she was much faster and more graceful, like a cat or a swan. It wasn't fair how amazing she was. I wanted to rip her head clean off her perfectly broad shoulders!

"Have you never fought a single person in your life?" Was it so obvious how I flailed about? I couldn't anticipate her movements. All I knew was to wildly swing, and she knew how to turn my wasted energy into her best friend. I did try a couple of punches and kicks, but she blocked and dodged those very well. It wasn't long until I was on my back, grunting and growling through my fangs.

"Tell me if he's alive!"

She had my hands restrained behind my back, and her body was holding me down. "You are a very strong girl, Jesse, but don't forget your place."

To make matters worse, the rest of the pack finished eating, and they came to watch the tail end of the fight. I really tried to force Cassandra off me then, but she kept squeezing my arm. I screamed and buried my nose in the dirt. I thought she was going to break something.

"That's enough." Rich was the only one with the courage to even say anything to her. He must have caught her off guard because he tossed Cassandra by her neck. He was lucky she thought it was funny and laughed instead of kicking his butt.

I was bummed about losing. Actually, I think I was furious and still heavily burdened by the urge to rip her head off. Rich helped me to my feet, but I tried to push through him to attack Cassandra once again. He was, unfortunately, strong enough to hold me back. Cassandra chuckled, and that just made me madder. Rich had to literally pull me away from everyone. I was determined to at least slap everybody who snickered. "You put up a good fight."

His compliment made me all mushy for some reason. I guess I was just seeking approval from my alpha. "Did I?"

"You did." Rich stared into my eyes and smiled. It seemed kind of sweet, but it sort of made me wanna throw up, and the feeling got worse when he plowed his lips into mine.

"Whoa!" I pushed him off me and let my tongue hang out. I wished I had one of those copper things used to scrape gunk off pans. I'm sure he must have been a good kisser to get Cassandra to make out with him, but his tongue touching mine was definitely a "wow" moment, but just in the direction of yuck. "What are you doing?"

I should have paid closer attention to his face. I probably hurt his pride. A lot. "You deserve to be queen of my pack."

I closed my mouth and touched my lips. What was so wrong with my life that my first two kisses were so atrocious? I was beginning to suspect my parents were making my love life miserable, so I would remain abstinent. I wouldn't be surprised if they were on their knees praying to God that my lady organs be like a skunk farm. "I'm glad you feel that way, but...I'm just not feeling this."

He fumed up his face and took his anger from a two to ten real quick. "Maxwell can't even touch you!"

"Not all relationships are about intimacy," I mumbled.

"Healthy ones involve it."

"Like what you have with Cassandra?"

He laughed and rolled his eyes. He was so arrogant; he probably chalked my hesitancy up to being wildly jealous. "We have an understanding. We don't have a relationship."

"She wants Maxwell to destroy you!"

"No. She wants Maxwell in the pack and under my thumb."

"If the prophecy was meant for Maxwell, she'll want more for him than a little destiny."

Rich jerked his head back and pressed his confused brows inward. "What prophecy?"

Jeez! I knew she was manipulating him like a puppet, but why would she tell me so much and not him? I was mixed somewhere between being socially awkward and super smug. "You might wanna talk to Cassandra. There's a lot more going on than her wanting to get your BFF in."

I tried to walk away from him, but he grabbed my arm and squeezed. "Why don't you tell me?"

I looked at his hand gripping me. It was clear from the way he tensed that he was really trying to hurt me and show his dominance, but the pain didn't bother me nearly as much as he aimed for. That pushed me more toward the smug side. "Remove your hand, or I'll break it off."

Rich breathed in and out slowly and heavily. He seemed like he was angry at first, but then he smirked and stepped closer to me. "You are so hot. I can't wait to imprint on you tonight."

"I doubt you're man enough, but good luck with that." I was able to push him off, and he smirked. He was really gonna go for it. Was it a wolfie rape thing? I think I should have been terrified, but I knew, without a shadow of a doubt, that I was going to send him away crying with his tail tucked between his legs.

I wondered if I would even have a tail...

Rich "allowed" me some alone time afterward. I just walked around the camp. There were a couple of guys who were supposed to be lookouts, but they weren't doing a very good job. They got distracted by our pretty girls very easily. I would have expected Cassandra to be bothered by their lack of focus, but maybe she didn't care about a perimeter, because she wanted to see Maxwell rip Rich's head off.

I wanted to worry about Maxwell, but I felt like it was a giant waste of time. Isn't that crazy, though? Why did I allow that much faith in him? I hadn't even seen him as a transitioning werewolf. How would our strange connection increase? Would it be like a bomb going off in my chest? If it did, my entire world was gonna go up in smoke. How would I be able to take him being human and me always remaining a monster? We couldn't be together, and I didn't wanna be selfish and ask him to be a werewolf for me. I'd have to learn to deal.

I kept looking up in the sky like it was suddenly gonna go dark and reveal an angry-faced moon emoticon. My hands and feet felt really strange, like they were numbing up or something. I could smell everything, which was nasty when someone wanted to pee in the woods. They could have flushed that crap while they were humanish! At least I wasn't being so bothered by my hunger. I felt pretty good since I ate that buffalo.

But the truth was, I didn't know if I would ever be able to get a true handle on my wolfiness. If I went home for Christmas, would I be able to stop myself from hurting my parents? And after I transformed, would I still love them the same way, or would I be racist like Rich? I would like to say I'd never be that crazy, but I honestly didn't know how different I'd be after I spent the night howling at the moon. I had to find a way to talk to them before the change. I wanted to hear their voice and feel deeply for them, like the way they felt for me.

If anyone was gonna help me, it was gonna be Stewart. I followed his scent and walked into the woods. He was hanging upside down in a tree. He was such an oddball, but I kind of liked that about him. I wished I had met him before we started craving people. I bet we would have laughed a lot.

"Hi, Stewart."

"Hey." He raised his legs, fell on his hands, and popped right up on his feet. He was up pretty high, but he seemed fine after he landed. "How are you?"

I shrugged, but then I decided to be honest with him. "I'm scared out of my mind about the transformation, and—"

"Can I imprint on you tonight?"

It got really quiet, and I know, because my hearing was off the charts, and I don't think anyone else in the entire world was talking. I blinked for a while, but then I just threw my head back and yelled, "Wow! Did you really just ask me that?"

My laugh probably didn't boost his confidence, but he apparently had more than he knew what to do with. "I didn't mean to. You're just very attractive right now, and everything is heightened. Some of the others are paring up right now, and I'd like to consummate, but if you'd like to wait until we transform—"

I grabbed Stewart by his neck, and I held him close to me, seething every word. "You can't even say the word 'sex' to my face, yet you have the audacity to ask me to be your mate?"

His eyes widened, and he gasped in fear of me. "I'm sorry—" That disgusted me more.

"You should be." After Steward was thrown to the ground, I realized I had changed more than I thought. I didn't know that I could say "sex" myself without blushing before, but I felt all tingly everywhere when I thought about it. My parents were very traditional. How would they feel if I wore a cream wedding dress because I was a slutty wolf during the full moon?

Stewart hesitantly stood up and wiped the dirt off his pants and shirt. "Did you want something from me?" He was too embarrassed to even look me in the eye.

I wanted to feel bad, but he should have sucked it up. He was one of Rich's favorites for a reason. I wasn't gonna tolerate him showcasing such weakness over nothing. "I want to call my parents before it's too late."

He shook his head and pressed his lips together firmly. "I could get into so much trouble!"

I narrowed my eyes on him and stepped closer. I tried to smile innocently, but I was empowered by the gulp he made, and I felt like my smile was pretty vicious. "Ask yourself one question: are you more afraid of Rich right now, or me?"

Stewart could be my friend. I'm sure he'd be a good subordinate if I had to take over the pack, but he would never imprint on me. "I'm gonna get your phone."

He rushed off to grab it, and I tried to calm down. Rich said I should be a queen, and Cassandra kept trying to suggest I should rule. Maybe it was something I had to genuinely consider. I didn't wanna be bossed around and told to kill and eat people. Maybe if I took control, I could almost have a normal life back. I could try. They'd have to help me!

Stewart came back in about five minutes and handed me my phone. Then, he handed me the SIM card. They probably disabled my GPS in my car, too. I noticed when I got inside, the navigator screen was black. My parents were probably freaking out. "Do you mind?"

"I shouldn't leave you completely alone. What if you call Maxwell?"

I didn't feel like arguing with him about why Maxwell didn't have a phone. He'd have to go far not to hear me anyway. "Just back up, will you?"

He did as he was told and jumped into the trees, but he was looking down on me. I thought Stewart was my friend, but it was clear the alpha truly did rule, and he was just another follower.

I took a deep breath and pressed the picture of my dad making a duck face. I had cropped his face, which was particularly hysterical. I couldn't imagine not seeing him ever again. I still loved him as much as I did before I got bitten. "Hey, Daddy."

"Jesse, where are you?" Uh oh. He was freaking out.

"I'm fine." I didn't wanna lie to him, but I consciously did. But honestly, my world didn't exactly feel like it was ending. "Don't worry about me."

"I am worried, sweetheart. You should be at the university by now. Where are you?"

"I'm taking some time to enjoy the land, Dad. I'll be in school and on time for orientation. I just need some space."

I heard Mom in the background. He quietly argued with her a little bit. I could tell from the sound of her voice that she was hysterically crying. Then, Dad put me on speakerphone. "I'm very sorry about all that you've been through. Your mother and I didn't mean to lie to you for all these years."

"But you did." If I had known their version of the truth, I felt like I would have been better prepared. Forcing me to live a fake life might have been compassionate, but it all seemed kind of pointless now. It was all ending too quickly.

"We only wanted to protect you!" Mom begged.

I wanted to tell my crying mother that I understood and thank them for their kindness, but the truth was, I was a little irritated. They didn't think I was strong enough to take the truth, or maybe they didn't respect me. I went to the apple orchard of fake grandparents. I was trapped inside my house—my whole entire life—not allowed to be social. I couldn't even mourn my brother or my friend, because their deaths were wrapped in such a mystery. They underestimated me, and I didn't want them to make me weak anymore. "I appreciate that, but now, I can take care of myself. Don't worry about me. I mean it."

"Jesse—"

I hung up on them. They were never going to let me go, and I didn't want them to convince me to come back home. I was still on the fence about who I should be and what I would do. Honestly, that was between my wolf and me now.

Stewart dropped down from below and looked at me, surprised. "That wasn't much of a goodbye."

I suddenly realized how cold I was, and I was concerned with how little it bothered me. "It was what it needed to be."

I think I wanted to be alone, but I could smell steaks sizzling on the grill. I joined the rest of the pack for a feast before the turn. I think someone raided the nearest party store; all we had was junk, meat, and booze. I wondered if they expected their wolfie powers to magically keep them in shape. If it didn't, they were gonna be real surprised when their thirties started them on a downward spiral.

Rich was still big brother enough to confiscate the beers from his siblings. They moaned, but he was strict, kept one for himself, and handed the other off to me. "You ready?"

I was not that stupid. Plying a woman with alcohol was all part of a boy's plan to get them naked and imprinted on. I passed my beer off to another girl, grinned hard in his face, and took my seat among the campfire where some wolves were roasting marshmallows.

Rachel came to sit beside me. It made me happy she was a normal teenager and wanted to eat fluffy calories, but Rachel did have a crazy look in her eye when she watched it toast and eventually burn. She just had too much…intention? She was aware of her surroundings, and she blew out the fire slowly like she knew someone might have gotten a rise out of it. I don't think it was a good idea to expose a little girl going through puberty to her sexual wolfie side. "Rich, can I turn a boy if I find someone I like?"

"No!" he shrieked. "You're too young for a mate."

"He doesn't have to imprint on me." But she kind of had a look on her face like she'd be the one doing the imprinting.

Rich pointed his finger right at his sister. "If anyone tries before you're twenty-one, they're dead."

"Twenty-one?" she laughed.

"Rich, that's extreme," Dennis chimed in.

"I'm just looking out for you two." He sat between them and started making s'mores. It was weird how tight-knit they were. When I looked around, though, they all kind of were. Even awkward Stewart was friendly with the female population, though his position was held firmly in the friend zone.

My heart was pounding. I thought about running through the woods with them. It seemed like it would be fun, and I struggled with keeping myself worried. If I were a part of their pack, they wouldn't hurt me. They'd even fight for me. I knew because, as freaked out as I was by Rachel, I wanted to protect her too. Was that me wanting to be a good person and look out for a kid, or was my secret desire to be a wolf queen peeking through? I'd either have to mate with Rich or kill him to make that happen, and I couldn't kill him. If I did, I'd become human.

That's what I wanted! I just couldn't take that away from Maxwell. I was sacrificing my humanity for his. That was all. I didn't wanna be a wolf. No way.

I got up and headed back to the woods. I wasn't thinking straight, so I needed to get away from the crazy wolf people and remember what I wanted out of life. I wanted to be a doctor.

Cassandra was stalking me and, of course, got up to follow. "Where are you going?"

"I need some air."

"I'll come with you."

"I said I need some air!" I snapped at her ferociously.

Cassandra chuckled, and that only made me more upset. I restrained myself, though. I didn't want to engage in a fight with her and feel even less like I should have. "It won't be much longer…" she sang.

She didn't have to remind me. I could already feel my blood surging. My muscles felt like they were turning into steel. I think my skin was itchy, but maybe that was my brain's way of telling me I was ready to just let what was inside of me bust through. My hunger was starting to come back, and the smells wouldn't stop. There was a farm miles away. I loved to go horseback riding when I was little, and I never forgot the distinct smell of the stables. The horses were probably going to die along with all the chickens, cows, and…goats? There were people, too. I already knew which one of them I wanted to kill.

I covered my mouth and trembled. My fangs were protruding, and I felt monstrous. I didn't want to hurt anyone. If this truly was a curse inflicted on those who committed atrocities, then how come good people like me could be infected? Why would God allow such a vicious virus to spread, and how come there was a part of me that welcomed it?

I began to pick up a scent lingering somewhere out in the woods. It was familiar, but it wasn't human. To me, the pack smelled a little bit like dogs, but it was obviously different. I don't think it would have been anything a human could notice. I mean, I never thought Maxwell smelled like anything when I was with him. But I suddenly remembered him smelling great.

"Maxwell?" Yes. That was the scent! It was like the scent of the wind carrying leaves. He always liked to run, and the wind was infused with his skin. Rich and Cassandra must have known his scent as well, so I ran toward Maxwell before it was too late to save him from getting jumped by the pack. In a couple of minutes, I could see him. "Maxwell!"

He was searching for something, and when he stepped from behind a tree and looked at me, I could tell by his smile that I was the one he had been searching for. "Jesse!"

My feet didn't know how to stop, and neither did my excitement. I just crashed into his chest and wrapped my arms around him for probably the biggest hug of his life. I think I was two seconds away from kissing him, too, but his fingers gripped my arms, and I was violently thrown off him. He started twitching oddly as he proceeded to wipe the touch of me from his face and arms.

"Sorry." I looked away, embarrassed. My instincts told me the wolf should have made me more attractive, and I hoped he could break through his phobia. "I was just so excited."

He freaked out a little bit longer, but he stopped before I wanted to ram my head into a tree. I did pick up the scent of blood, and then I noticed the scratch mark on his chest. "What did they do to you?" I started reaching out to touch him, but I pulled my hand away. It sucked that I could probably hurt him worse than the scratch.

"I handled Rich's lackeys. Don't worry about me. I heal fast."

I was worried, but if he could overcome two vicious werewolves, he could take the little alpha. After all, he was the boy of prophecy. He was smart, strong, and kind. He was loyal. If he wanted to stay a werewolf, he would have made a remarkable pack leader. I could sense it.

I stopped looking at his scratch and looked at his face. He was sniffing at me, and I started sniffing at him. It was quite weird, but it was kind of amazing at the same time. We stepped closer to each other and continued to smell the fragrance of each other's skin. It's like the more I could smell him, the more I could remember his little face from next door. I could see his chubby face laughing with my brother, Kevin, as they ran around the yard. But no one could keep up with Kevin. He was stronger and faster than all of us.

"They turned you, didn't they?" he asked while very close to my lips.

"They did." I was trying very hard not to kiss him, but I felt like I was falling into the ocean with weights on my legs. I don't know if I was physically rocking back and forth, but it didn't feel like I was standing still.

Maxwell breathed heavily. He remained strong and stayed away from humans, but he finally hit a bump in the road when it came to his resolve. "This feels very intense right now. Do you feel this?"

"I do." My blood was rushing, and I felt tingly all over again. I wanted to touch him so bad, but I was trying to be respectful. "I don't wanna be drawn to you just because our wolves wanna mate. That's not how I imagined I'd meet my husband."

"I agree…" His eyes changed into gold, and the wolf's eyes never became so gorgeous to me as they were at that moment. He looked super-hot.

"But you're wolfing out on me."

"You are too." I think the wolf really took over because he grabbed my face and pulled me into his lips. My tingles became more like burning sensations, and my arms found their way around his broad shoulders. I had never felt such a rush of life flowing through my body. The rightness of our union was so massive that it forced the rest of the universe to circle us. Even though I didn't know Maxwell before, I knew that tasting his lips was something I wanted to do my entire life. That's how kisses were supposed to feel!

I think he growled somewhere in between the kisses. I must have been into it because I growled back. At some point, I sort of jumped on top of him and wrapped my legs around his waist. He rested up against a tree and kissed my neck and shoulders. His touch was incredible—a hundred times better than a massage—but when I decided I wanted to kiss him there, to make him feel my glorious sensations, he sent me flying into the ground.

"Sorry." He wiped down his lips, face, and everywhere else I touched him. I guess that also included his chest and neck. His eyes returned to normal, and he rocked back and forth like he was totally going to vomit again.

"No. It's good you're still yourself." I turned away as I stood up and fought off tears. I knew it wasn't his fault, but it was so not an awesome feeling to cause someone you care about pain by being with them.

And, of course, he stood behind a tree and puked out whatever delicious burger he had for lunch. He was breathing heavily and shaking. I don't remember if this was my imagination or not, but I think his eyes might have even been glistening. "Even this weak part of me?"

"I don't think you're weak." Even with what he was, and what we apparently couldn't do, I couldn't see him that way. He had gone an entire month clean. I don't know how he managed not to bite me in the car if he felt, even a little bit, of the way I felt for him now.

"Have you killed any humans?"

"No. I swear I haven't." I was too ashamed to tell him about what almost happened. I didn't even wanna tell him about the buffalo. I felt like a sellout for even asking for Stewart's help or running with the pack.

"Good." He was still intensely and supernaturally drawn to me. He started reaching out to touch my face. I braced myself for his delicate touch, but he never quite made it. His fingers trembled, and he pulled away. "You have to kill Rich."

"Me?" I laughed and shook my head. "No. I can't let you give away your only shot at humanity for me. I should have been careful. It's my own fault."

"I should have never left you alone in that hotel. I should never have gotten in your car in the first place. I just didn't know you and I would have such a connection. I should have caught a bus as soon as I knew I wanted you."

"And how long ago was that?" I asked curiously.

He smiled and placed his fidgety fingers in his pockets. "The moment I saw you hiding in your car."

I smiled widely, and I don't know why I started crying. It just felt very satisfying, especially since he kept vomiting every time I kissed him. "I've known for much longer."

"Oh, really?" He cocked his brow, and that made him even cuter.

"From the moment you defended me against Annie…" I could see her running to the porch and him grabbing her shoulders. He looked irritated and pointed my way. Annie pouted and ran inside the house. Maxwell looked at me and shrugged his shoulders. I think I smiled at him, but he went back inside the house. I looked down at the chalk and gripped it tightly. "…but I think I did steal her chalk."

He threw his head back and laughed. "You're remembering me?"

"Not a whole lot, but I do know some things." I had a sense that I was so sad when we moved away. I knew Kevin and Annie were gone. I vaguely remembered their funerals. I think I remembered trying to hug Maxwell, but he pulled away and cried. I felt awful, but now, I know it was the beginning of his haphephobia forming. I remembered seeing him in his backyard and watching from my window a few times. He seemed so miserable. Then, we left soon afterward. Things sort of became a blur after that, but I don't think anyone called me Jessica anymore. I think I still missed Maxwell, even if I couldn't quite remember him. Geez, I was crushing hard from the age of three!

"If we never suffered the tragedy of losing Annie and Kevin, you probably would have grown up and had a lot of girlfriends. I would have been too shy to speak up, but Annie probably would have pestered me every day about confessing my feelings. Knowing me, I would probably wait for some super inconvenient time like your wedding day." I laughed at the pathetic scenario I whipped up in my head. "I'd totally be in the wedding party, wouldn't I?"

"Probably right next to Annie," he laughed as well, and he had such a beautiful smile.

"Would you hate me forever for ruining your big day?" I don't know why I felt guilty about it.

"Hypothetically speaking?" His smirk had a little shame mixed in. "I probably wouldn't have realized how radiant you looked until the night before. You'd probably wear some exquisite dress to the rehearsal dinner." He was staring as if he could see me in it already. "I think I'd feel like a creeper at first, but then, I'd come to grips with the fact you were an adult."

I squealed a little bit. I wanted to live in that movie moment. Couldn't we take our lives back? "Would we kiss?"

"I don't know."

"We would. I would overstep my boundaries. Annie would see it." I covered my face as if she were about to catch us.

"She always did like to snoop."

I really wanted to be with Maxwell, but I felt a little unworthy. I wasn't willing to do what I needed to keep him. One of us was gonna end up as a human. Then, it'd be all over between us. "I don't know if I'd have the courage to speak out at the altar, though."

"I wouldn't have made it to the altar," he insisted quickly. "When I realize what I want, I go after it."

"Good." His steely gaze was giving me chills. "I didn't wanna run away with a groom. A fiancé is okay."

I could tell Maxwell wanted to be happy with me, but I also knew he was afraid. He held his hand up with his palm toward me. I did the same and waited for him to gather the courage to touch me, but the closer his skin got to mine, the more his hand trembled. He gritted his teeth in hatred and shame at how he was. I silently cheered him on. I knew he could overcome his phobia, but it was painful to watch. He looked like he was holding his hand in a fire and trying not to get burned. I didn't wanna see him upset, so I pulled my hand away first.

He looked at his hand and sneered as if it were diseased. "I'm still broken, Jesse. I can't stand to touch you as long as I'm like this. I know it's difficult, but it's the way I am."

"I don't mind!"

He cocked his brow. "Really?"

I snickered. He made me feel like I was naughty, but I genuinely liked him. "I mean, I mind, but you're worth it. I know you are."

He kind of had a naughty smile, too, but then he got serious. "I'll challenge Rich, and when the time is right, I'll let you kill him."

He was so sweet. I knew he'd lay his humanity at the altar for me, but I couldn't let him lose anything else. "I'd much rather have you break the curse for yourself."

"Don't argue about this with me, Jesse."

"Seriously, I don't mind."

He jerked his head back and furrowed his brows. "You don't mind?"

"That's not what I meant," I stammered. "I wish I were still human, but I guess I'm not as bothered about it as you are..." I hadn't realized it until the words escaped my mouth, but I honestly didn't want to be cured. How intensely I felt for Maxwell was the nail in my humanity's coffin. I really could love like a penguin. "I can live with it."

I wanted him to see. I needed him to, but he seemed afraid for me. "Jesse, what have they done to you?"

"She's come to realize her place," Cassandra said from behind. I watched Maxwell's face become more enraged the closer she got to us. I didn't move, though, not even when Cassandra placed her hand on my shoulder. "Now, it's time for you to realize yours."

Chapter Twelve

Maxwell was about to lunge out—to do what, I'm not sure—but he stopped when Stewart emerged from the trees. Little Stewart was tough, but he wasn't strong enough to beat Maxwell. He wasn't alone, though. Others ran from the camp, and Maxwell couldn't fight an army. He didn't have a choice.

I walked beside Maxwell as we escorted him to the camp, but he refused to look at me. Why was he so upset? I didn't understand how he could hate the incredible power we felt. How could he despise the shock of power in his legs when his feet pounded on the ground? How could he hate the rush of catching a whiff of my skin in the wind? Or the anticipation of seeing me again? Somewhere along the way, he stopped following Rich's scent and looked for me.

I don't think I wanted to stop being a doctor or stop loving my parents, but I did like feeling powerful and desirable. Even though Cassandra handed my butt to me on a silver platter, I still felt invincible. I felt like I was up to the challenge of taking on anyone else in the pack. Despite Maxwell's puke fest, I still felt incredibly sexy. I never felt that way before, and I didn't want it to stop. Plus, how scrumptious hearts were was a bonus. I didn't wanna hurt anyone, but I did wanna tear into another animal heart. How could Maxwell not wanna give being a werewolf a fair shot?

I wished he would stop being angry with me! I was not on Rich's side. I wanted Maxwell to take his place. We wouldn't have to kill people and have wild parties every night when he was in charge. We could have the community without the scariness. I had to be as naïve as possible and believe there was a chance at being decent monsters.

I looked up at the sky. It was beginning to get darker. Maxwell was certainly cutting things close. "I believe in you, Maxwell."

"I'm sorry I can't save both of us." He was still too angry to look at me, but I appreciated his sentiment.

However, I wasn't sure I wanted to be saved, or that I needed him to do it anyway.

Rich stood on a huge rock with his hands outstretched. He was smiling like he didn't know exactly what Maxwell planned to do. "Maxwell! I'm kind of surprised to see you."

With our arrival, the pack was complete, besides the two Maxwell supposedly killed. Even if I helped Maxwell, he was still at a disadvantage. However, Maxwell never let his confidence waver. "You can't assassinate me, Rich. I'm gonna kill you in front of your pack."

There were not so silent whispers from among the crowd of wolves.

"Is that a formal challenge for leadership?" Cassandra could have tried a little bit harder to hide her mischievous intentions.

"If it's not, we'll have to rip you apart," Rich said. "We don't tolerate outside threats well." Rich stayed calm physically, but the rest of the pack growled and began to tense up. I saw a flash of gold shoot across the camp as they all prepared themselves to defend the pack. I didn't really want to strike out at Maxwell, but I could feel my eyes changing.

"Jesse…?" Maxwell seemed disappointed, but he wasn't sure of my intentions.

I did feel protective of the pack, but I also felt protective of Maxwell. I honestly wasn't sure what I was about to do. "Challenge him for leadership, Maxwell. A wolf has to belong to a pack."

He cut his eyes at me, and I shut my mouth tight. I was only trying to help! "Fine, Rich. I formally challenge you for alpha status."

Rich grinned hard and jumped off his rock. "We'll do it after the transformation—"

"Alphas don't wait," Cassandra said, offended. "Alphas demonstrate their power whenever they need to. You have to fight him now."

Not everyone understood Cassandra's relationship with Rich (especially Rich himself), but she knew more stuff about what was proper for a werewolf. Now that she called Rich out, he would seem like a little punk if he didn't come right out and fight Maxwell.

Rich gave Cassandra one heck of a death glare, and she gave him a devious smile in return. I think they might have had a mild conversation about the prophecy. Rich wasn't as cocky as I thought he would be.

"He'd never fight Maxwell," I said with a smirk. "Rich knows Maxwell would win."

Rachel practically lunged at me. She would have torn my eyes out if it weren't for her brother holding her back. "My brother isn't afraid of Maxwell. He'll take him out right here and now!"

Rich glared at his sister, and she silenced herself. I'm sure he would have punished her for talking out of turn, but he'd have to live through the next few minutes. But she and Cassandra had put him into quite the predicament. There was no waiting until the full moon to see if Maxwell would change his mind about seeking revenge. His humanity was lost. He had to act now if he wanted to keep our respect.

Rich shook his head and laughed. He probably felt like the king of all fools, but he was too delusional not to try. "Fine, brother, we'll fight." Rich prepared for battle by removing his T-shirt, and he sure was sculpted.

My head snapped to Maxwell. I really hoped he was into the ultra-sexy fight thing too, but he didn't take off his shirt. I guess that didn't make sense with his touching people phobia, but a girl could dream.

I did worry about him, though. I could tell he was angry and focused, but he also looked a little pale. I wasn't sure if he could overcome his haphephobia long enough to defeat Rich, and the setting sun probably didn't help with Maxwell's anxiety.

We all made space for them instinctively, and they circled around each other in the sphere we created. Cassandra stood upon the giant rock to get a better look at the bloodshed. I wanted to look away, but I was also excited about it, in a creepy way. I was watching my king be made, and I was very ready for him.

Rich had this wicked swagger to his walk, like a discount villain from an 80's action flick. "I must warn you, Maxwell, you will regret crossing me."

"All my regret went out of the window when you killed my mother."

Rich shrugged and cruelly smirked. "Well, at least she tasted good."

Maxwell growled and rushed in to strike Rich, but he sort of lost his nerve when he got too close. His monster strike slowed down enough for Rich to gain the upper hand, and he ducked from Maxwell's punch and elbowed him in the face. Maxwell staggered back, and Rich took the opportunity to punch him a couple of more times. I remembered seeing some pictures of Rich and Maxwell at a gym together, boxing. I never saw Maxwell fighting someone, though. This was really bad! I didn't know Rich could actually fight.

Maxwell took a couple of steps back and wiped his face with his arm. He was trying his best not to freak, but I knew Maxwell well enough to recognize him wigging out. Unfortunately, Rich knew him a lot better than I did.

Rich laughed and ran to shove his fingers in his face. Maxwell wasn't fast enough to dodge, and he got super invaded. He had a very volatile reaction and practically scrubbed his face off. There was no way to hide that from everyone.

"He's always been weak," Dennis said to his sister. "He's a fool to think he could defeat our brother."

I wanted to hurt those brats for their lack of respect. I knew Maxwell looked like a total freak, but he was my freak, and he was going to be alpha soon.

"You are so pathetic!" Rich mocked. "How do you expect to run my pack when you're crippled by fear?"

I was really worried about him. He had no color in his face, and his entire body was trembling. But even though he was a total weirdo, I had an irrational and unshakable faith in him. I didn't think it was a good idea to voice my treason for Rich out loud, but I didn't care. "You can do it, Maxwell! Rip his head off!"

I think my rabid cheering must have triggered something in him. He warned me once that his phobia could cripple him, but he also said it could force him to go into full-on crazy mode. Rich went after Maxwell again, but he was totally taken off guard when Maxwell howled like a crazy person and started swinging back.

Maxwell was quick. Most of his sports involved running, and he was used to dodging people. When Rich tried to hit him, Maxwell was already two steps ahead of him. Maxwell plowed his knuckles repeatedly into Rich's skull. He yelled like a monster in pain, but I think it had a lot to do with the fact that Rich's blood splattered on his face.

"This is the fight I've been waiting for…" Cassandra's mouth was practically watering. "He's wonderful, exactly what I expected."

Rich backed off and spat up a mouthful of blood. Maxwell came wildly at Rich again, but he was ready for Maxwell and flipped him over in front of him. Rich put Maxwell in a headlock, and Maxwell was suddenly snapped back to a reality where he wasn't a lunatic wildly fighting. He was being touched, which meant he was being smothered by innumerable pains.

"What's the matter?" Rich asked in Maxwell's ear. "Did you not make the wrestling team in high school with me?" Maxwell struggled to rip Rich's arm off him, but Rich started wolfing out to make sure he'd be strong enough to keep Maxwell on lockdown. "This is your worst fear, isn't it? Being touched?"

Maxwell began to panic. He beat on Rich's arm instead of trying to pry it off. He had so much anxiety that he could barely breathe, and it was worse that Rich was going to choke him out, especially when he screamed.

"I have to do something. I have to…" I probably shouldn't have muttered to myself out loud.

"You can't." Cassandra dropped down from the rock, grabbed my shoulder, and squeezed. "This is between the two of them. If you interfere, Rich will remain the alpha, and you will both bow to him."

I pulled on my hair because I really wanted to rip it out. Rich would never allow a union between Maxwell and me to stand. And I would have much rather caused Maxwell to vomit after my pleasurable and painful kisses, than for me to puke up my guts because Rich revolted me. "You have to do something!"

Maxwell was doing his best not to allow the wolf to take over his life. He wanted to prove he could be stronger and overcome it with his sheer willpower, but Rich had already embraced who he was. There was a wolf fighting a human, and that was unfair. A fight for alpha could only be between two wolves.

Maxwell closed his eyes and took a very deep breath. The paleness of his skin began to, oddly, fade back into color. His screams and whimpers quieted into subtle growls. He gritted his teeth, hissed, and breathed through his clenched jaws. When he opened his eyes back up, they were golden.

Oh, it was so on. "Get him!"

Maxwell was suddenly strong enough to pull Rich's arm right off. He maneuvered behind Rich and pulled that jerk's arm behind his body. Rich was totally surprised, and it was awesome when Maxwell pulled, and I heard the bone snap. Maxwell was so brutal, and it was kind of hot.

"Is this really happening?" Stewart asked, amazed. "Is Rich really going to lose?"

Rich was in genuine pain—the girlish screams made it obvious—but he was a trooper. He powered out of it in some kind of fast and cool wrestling-type move. He tried to get Maxwell back on the ground, but he was faster and stronger and popped right back up.

"What's the matter, Rich? You can't take the beast you created?"

"I'm just glad to see you embrace who you are, finally." I thought Rich was a punk, but he grabbed his bad shoulder and popped it back into place. Considering how much I cringed from the sound of his bone inserting back into its socket, I must admit, it was hardcore. "You can see the gift I've given you?"

"I do, and in return, I'll grant you a swift death." The only way to let go of his fear of touch was to let go of himself and fall deeper into the wolf persona. Rich tried to swipe his claws against Maxwell's chest and face, but he moved as if he could anticipate Rich's movements. I didn't know if Maxwell had a special sense like Stewart's ability to climb so well, but he was certainly built for some advantage. Rich couldn't even touch him anymore.

"No way," Stewart said under his breath.

"Should we do something?" Dennis asked.

Rachel slashed her slightly older brother in the face and growled at him for even suggesting such a thing. "Don't you dare interfere! This is our brother's moment of glory, whether he lives or dies."

I still wasn't sure if I wanted that crazy wolf girl in my pack. Each moment, she found a new way to terrify me in the "chop me up into pieces while I slept" kind of way.

But Rich's siblings had a right to be worried. Ever since they went beast mode, they were wild and ferocious things swiping their hands across each other's chests and faces with the grace of a bear, but Maxwell gained more humanistic control with each second. Rich felt the brunt of it when he charged Maxwell and met a roundhouse kick to the face.

"I thought this guy had some kind of phobia about touching," one of the guys said.

"That doesn't mean he didn't learn how to kick butts!" I raised my fists in the air and squealed in excitement. Maxwell landed another punch in Rich's face. He was extremely active growing up, so it made sense that he knew how to fight. If Maxwell could think at all in his beast mode, I bet he probably felt like he could finally put on a performance that he had prepared for his entire life.

"It won't be too long," Cassandra dropped her head back, raised her hands to the sky, and basked in the glow of the oncoming night. "We'll all change soon."

"You have to hurry!" I screamed.

But I don't think Maxwell could hear me. He was a full-blown wolf machine, programmed for one mission: to destroy Rich. Rich tried to punch Maxwell, and he yelled in frustration from each easily deflected blow. It was like watching an adult slap the hand of a greedy child. Maxwell grabbed his arms and began to squeeze. That's when I really didn't recognize him. I mean, it was cool he wasn't screaming from mental pain, but the cruel laugh was a bit much. It was kind of getting to the point where I was a little afraid.

"Max...?" Rich fell to his knees, and he struggled to contain girlish screams as Maxwell crushed his arms. "Max. Max, stop!"

A malevolent grin spread across Maxwell's face as he twisted and squeezed his victim. "Submit."

The pain on Rich's face and the screech in his voice made everything so intense. "Max, I can't—"

"Then, you die."

Our instincts barely gave us time to jump clear of Rich's body, flinging into the giant rock. I was so sure he was dead. His limp body rested in the split boulder. His skull was fractured, and his eyes fluttered. He coughed, and chunks of blood spewed like a geyser. Wolves healed fast, but that totally looked like a bad sign.

The kids cried, even Ms. Invincible Rachel. I couldn't blame them. I must have cried when my brother died.

I felt like I was losing somebody, though. Maxwell wasn't the same Good Samaritan who fixed my tire. He had a confident and creepy death aura walk about him, and it was kind of horrible. It was still attractive, but scary. He had this murderous smirk—like he was about to make out with a death god—and his wolfie features seemed accentuated. Maxwell's cold eyes pierced through the oncoming darkness, and his voice lowered an octave. "Submit."

Rich couldn't speak, but we all felt a shift. Rich had nothing left to give, and we fell in submission to our new leader. Even the children easily dropped to their knees, despite the pure horror in their young and foolish eyes.

The only wolf standing was the obvious puppet master, pleased with her pack. "I am so proud of you, Maxwell."

Chapter Thirteen

With Rich being a non-threat, Maxwell turned his monster vibes toward the only wolf who would openly defy him. Cassandra never even flinched when it came to Rich, but she sweated in Maxwell's presence. He could probably smell her fear because I sure could. He fed off it like a drug. "You should kneel with the rest of them."

She grinned hard and erupted into a nervous chuckle, while backing away. "I concede to your monstrous strength, certainly, but my maker is far above you on the power ladder. You have no idea!"

She was like a proud mother looking at her grown-up baby boy. Except that's totally a horrible metaphor. I'm certain she would have bedded Maxwell the same way she did Rich. She had a certain smugness about her, as if she were his god, bragging about how well her creation turned out. That's a more appropriate way to look at it, especially if she were like a frisky Greek god. "I couldn't bow to you even if I wanted to. If you want power over someone like me, you must defeat stronger pack leaders. It's usually suicide, but you're special. Is that something you want?"

I didn't trust her before, but it was a hundred times worse now. But the most terrible thing was that he seemed intrigued by the power he didn't want before. "Maxwell?" I ran to his side, and he only glanced at me like he barely knew me.

"Don't you feel the urge to rule this pack?" Her temptress lips were a little too close to his ears. She spoke so seductively; I thought she might have a nibble of him. "Don't you feel the urge to go on and become more? You were always the child of prophecy. It was never Kevin."

Rachel and Dennis fought off tears, but poor Dennis couldn't hold his tongue while his brother's skull oozed blood. "Rich needs help!"

"Your brother is lost!" Maxwell snapped. "He's going to die."

I almost felt pity for the children. They didn't seem like monsters anymore. They were just scared kids caught in something they shouldn't have messed with. I understood and agreed with killing Rich to preserve Maxwell's humanity, but he didn't strike me as a revenge person before.

Cassandra looked up. The sun had set. The sky was continuously darkened, but the full moon had yet to reveal itself to us. "Maxwell, if you kill Rich right now, you become a human. You would forsake your nature and allow Jesse to live cursed without you?"

I grabbed Maxwell's hands to see if he would pull away, but he didn't. He was still so much of the wolf, and he could see what I had seen. In a way, that excited me. I was honored to have him be my alpha, and I was dying inside to be his queen. He inhaled my scent again, and I accidentally got a big whiff of him too. Maxwell bent down and tenderly kissed my neck. I returned the favor, and he didn't pull away. My wolf wanted him to imprint on me, and the practical human part of me knew we were rushing things, but he was gonna totally be good in bed.

But there was still a bigger human part in me, and she remembered how much Maxwell didn't want to be a werewolf. I respected that part of him, even if he couldn't exactly remember it. I wouldn't be able to live with myself if the real Maxwell didn't choose. "Maxy...?"

As I took in the scent of him, I remembered the distinct dusty smell of a basement and sewage from flooded pipes. I also remembered the scent of Maxwell's young skin as I looked down on him. I was bleeding. I scratched my knee on a little window. I didn't want to leave him, but he couldn't reach the top, and I was too tiny to pull him up. He pushed me through, and I wasn't strong enough to repay his kindness.

There was another smell there. I think I was too little to comprehend, but I didn't wanna leave Maxwell alone to fend for himself. We were both terrified.

"Kevin made me promise I would always protect you." He pulled away from me. He was still wolfie, but at least he was more tamed. "I protected you back then, didn't I?"

"You did." I tried to remember more, including Kevin, but Maxwell's skin triggered flashes of him holding me and telling me everything would be alright. "You're why I escaped. You're the only reason why I'm alive."

"And I want to keep protecting you, Jesse." His natural eye color returned, and his canine teeth receded into his gums. He meant to hold me with declawed hands, but he couldn't. He was his hopeless, quirky, and selfless self again. "You need to kill Rich and become human."

"No!" I wanted to scream at him, but the fact that he was my alpha reduced me to a pathetic whimper. "You can't be serious. You want me to give this up? You want me to give you up?"

Maxwell's eyes glossed up. He raised his head to keep the tears in, and he smiled in amusement at his own weakness. "Everything I ever had is gone. You still have so much to live for as a human. Your parents will never give up on you, not unless you fake your death."

As cruel as that sounded, it was still an option. "Well—"

"If you fake your death, you can't go to that college you've been dying to get to. You'll never be a doctor. Don't you want a normal life? Don't you want kids and a husband who doesn't …shed?" he laughed with a hint of hysteria.

I left my parents to change. I wanted to be strong and independent. I didn't want to succumb to peer pressure and give my whole life away to be with a man I barely knew. Was I reinventing myself, or was I selling out? "We won't shed, will we?"

I was glad I could still make him laugh in the face of the rottenest night of our lives. It made me curious if I could make him happy forever. You know? Through sickness and health, richer or poorer, etc.…

"If Annie and Kevin truly were killed because I was born to have this curse, then I'd rather just be cursed if I can spare you from my fate."

"You don't deserve this!" I didn't wanna cry in front of him, especially not in front of our pack. I had such an ugly cry face.

"I don't care about what I deserve. I care about what's right." He surprised me when I felt his fingers graze mine. I was gonna pull away from shock, but I was curious if he could finally trust me enough to let me feel him. "I'm sorry it's taken so long to know how I feel about you."

"It's only been a few days."

His fingers shivered, but he took a deep breath and locked his pinky with mine. "It feels like a lifetime."

He was just too cute! Screw penguins. He was forever my epic love. "You don't have to do this, Maxwell."

"I'm afraid I have to." He raised his hand with our pinkies still intertwined. Then, he kissed his hand. I kissed mine as well. It wasn't exactly what I imagined our last kiss to be like, but it felt kind of perfect. I could smile through my insanely ugly tears.

My nervous system surged like I had been struck by lightning, and my blood was boiling. Was I turning into a werewolf or a freaking dragon? It felt pretty cool before, but now, it hurt.

"You're running out of time, Jesse. You have to do it now."

I reluctantly let go of his hand and walked to Rich. He was probably going to die anyway. I told myself I shouldn't feel bad about ending him. Honestly? I didn't need to tell myself that, even if his siblings had to watch. The only awkward part was that he was barely conscious, and I didn't defeat him. It didn't seem very honorable to take Maxwell's leftovers.

I guess all Rich could do was smile in the face of death. "I didn't see this coming, but I'm not exactly surprised."

I cracked my knuckles and summoned my ferocious claws. It was the end of my wolfie journey. Who was to say I wouldn't be overcome with guilt once I destroyed him?

But wolf me still wanted him dead. "You brought this on yourself." I really put some force into my swipe to ensure he wouldn't survive. His flesh caught inside my nails, and his blood flowed down the rock and splattered all over me, and a couple of other wolves wanted to witness his death, like Stewart. Rich's brother and sister whimpered, but they were troopers. The loudest reaction was perhaps the quietest: the smack of Cassandra's lips when she pressed them together for a smirk.

"You have to run," Maxwell pleaded. "We won't be able to control ourselves, and we're close to changing."

But I didn't want to ever leave him. I didn't feel our connection wane. My senses didn't dull. As a matter of fact, they were still getting sharper. I didn't feel any sort of discomfort from Rich's blood on my hands. "I don't feel different."

"Maybe it'll take time. Just go!"

Wouldn't it be horrible if he freed me just to turn loose and kill me? But I didn't feel like prey. I knew from the moment I pressed my tongue against that heart, I would never feel that way again. I wouldn't run away simply because he was terrified for my safety. It was insulting. "I wanna stay with you, Maxwell."

He stepped closer and looked into my eyes in complete, horribly awful shock. "You're still wolfing out."

I couldn't say I was disappointed. I would have hated to feel fear when I looked into his golden eyes. "Maybe the cure was a lie."

Maxwell's eyes widened as he had the atrocious revelation that turned into captivating rage. "Why would you lie?"

Cassandra acted quickly and jumped several feet away from Maxwell, but she was unexpectedly slashed in the back by Rachel, and she got her good. "You put a death sentence on my brother's head for no reason!"

Rachel and Dennis were insane trying to attack Cassandra, but I couldn't blame them. In a few seconds and with minimal moves, she had them both on the ground with bloodied faces, and she didn't even have a wrinkle in her clothes to show for it. "When you make a werewolf, you run the risk that someone is gonna be pissed about it. Your brother made a lot of enemies on his quest for power, and the stronger he became, the more vulnerable he made himself. If you kill your maker before your full transition, you stop the curse."

"Then why didn't it work?" Maxwell was so furious that his entire body shook when he yelled. I think he was trying hard not to wolf out, but there was no point anymore.

"Because she was already a full-fledged werewolf!"

Maxwell suffered from an invisible slap in the face, and his glare landed right on me. "You said you never killed anyone."

"I didn't!" I even tried hard to think about it. The only person I got close to killing died by her hand. "I was close, but—"

"It's not the kill," Cassandra said with a smile. "It's the heart."

But I saw Maxwell eat animal hearts, and he was still himself. If he could get away with hunting an innocent stray down, then why was I a monster because I had refrigerated buffalo…?

I remembered the way I felt after I bit into it: completely and wonderfully whole. I really felt my wolf for the first time, and instead of it chasing me, I wanted to chase her.

"Stewart…" I was enraged to the point of quivering. I thought he was my friend, yet I was about to make him just as dead as Rich. "Did I eat a buffalo heart?"

"Don't take it personally!" Little Stewart slowly backed away, but the other wolves blocked his path. "Rich made me do that to everyone who hesitated. Once you see what the wolf has to offer, you never let go."

I ruined everything. How could I be so stupid? I knew that was human blood. I could smell it. I tasted it! I didn't care. I only wanted to feed, and he put me in that situation. "I'll kill you!"

"Why?" Cassandra ran in between us so fast; she was like a blur. "He did you a favor!" I had no doubt Rich's clever lie was her idea. She might have beaten me before, but I was certainly up to the challenge!

I could sense the danger from all around. Cassandra was gonna be tough, but Rachel was really upset. "You killed my brother for no reason?"

"There were definitely reasons!" Three. I could take three werewolves, couldn't I? Two of them were kids.

But my greatest threat didn't make itself known until I heard his beastly growl, and I felt his hand wrap around my wrist. "I lasted an entire month without giving in to temptation and eating a human heart, and you couldn't even wait more than three days?"

Four werewolves? I definitely couldn't take four, especially if one was my alpha. I couldn't let him forget the true enemy. "I'm sorry, Maxwell, but this is Cassandra's fault. She wanted us both to turn!"

"And it's good to have you both officially a part of my team." Again, she reclaimed her spot on top of the rock. It seemed extremely disrespectful to Rich since she hovered above his mutilated body. Why would she care about respect, though? He was always her puppet, and we weren't any better. How much did she know about our past, and what exactly did she think Maxwell and I would become? "I hope you enjoy your first moon. It's always a doozy."

I looked at Maxwell, and he had already started stomping his feet into the ground on his way to snapping her neck. "I'll kill you—" He staggered off his feet and onto his knees, screaming in agony.

"Maxwell?" I rushed to him. I looked up at the sky and finally saw the dreaded yellow glow of an ominous full moon. It wasn't the angry emoticon I pictured. It was lovely. Its rays bathed my skin in radiance and began to simmer my insides, while it ripped apart Maxwell. "What's happening to him?"

"The strong usually change first. He's leading the charge." I caught Cassandra's top flying off from my peripheral vision. She stripped her clothes, and so did the other wolves. Some of them were bold and fearlessly prepared, while others were conservative, and their fingers trembled. The children were particularly afraid.

I turned my back on them. I didn't care about their stupid camaraderie or their code. I didn't wanna run with those traitors, and I didn't want to hunt with them either. They were the reason Maxwell was in pain. "Maxwell…?"

I had seen his eyes, teeth, and hands wolf out before, but this was different. He hunched over and held his chest as if an alien were going to pop right through it. I heard bones pop, break, and reform, and I totally wanted to retreat into nowhere. I felt helpless. I couldn't stop the transformation, and I couldn't even hold him and tell him everything was gonna be okay.

Cassandra screeched next. She really wasn't kidding about the order of the transformation, but she had this creepy laugh mixed in with her scream. She disgusted me so much! There was no more being sexy and charming. There was only the beast, and hers was just as ugly as anyone else's.

My surprise didn't arrive until a few seconds later. "Ow! Ow! Ow!" I could feel my bones shifting inside of me. I threw my top off, so I could see my rib cage expanding through my skin. I tried to unclasp the bra with my abnormally long hands, but the best I could do was to shred it off with claws.

Maxwell's body was growing and ripping through his shirt. His mouth was an arsenal of sharp teeth, and his face elongated into a snout. He stood up and hollered at the moon with the rest of the transforming pack. I think the sweet Maxwell was gone and replaced with the beast who overcame Rich. They weren't even screams of pain anymore. He was making a declaration over his territory and letting humans, animals, and other creatures that went bump in the night know that he would kill anyone who tried to lay claim to what belonged to him.

The weakness of my humanity faded away, and all I had left were my laser beam instincts. I don't think I screamed anymore. Pain was irrelevant when weighed against the power flowing through my body. I could already smell my first kill, and I knew exactly who I was going to run with. I didn't plan on making myself easy for him, but I could smell the perfect place where I wanted him to imprint on me, near a vegetable garden on a little farm. Then, I would be made the queen of the pack. The human part of me should have fought harder to squeeze in fear and remorse, but she was withering away. There was a real reason why Maxwell and I were taken as children. I think I was born ready for this.

Change.

Most people hate it, but I couldn't. I welcomed it. I craved it. I was supposed to fear the unknown, but I had taken Fate custody, and I was bending her to my will. I was not a victim of the night, nor a slave to the moon. Finally, I could run free with wild abandonment and truly take control of my life with the strength of a real queen.

It was gonna be amazeballs!

Dear Reader,

Thank you for your invaluable support! I extremely enjoy the process of writing, and I will continue until I am nothing but a memory, living on through the lips of my loved ones. The only satisfaction greater than completing a novel is the euphoria that overwhelms my heart when someone tells me they read and loved my story.

I ask that you consider leaving a review on websites like Amazon, Goodreads, your personal blog, and wherever else readers may gather. There is no greater advertisement than word of mouth, and reviews are the lifeblood of my business.

I write because I feel compelled to. I have dozens of stories and hundreds of characters trying to break through the borders of my brain. I wouldn't stop writing, one way or another, but it is an amazing accomplishment to know that someone else heard and appreciated the voice of these characters.

If this were a story worth reading, let someone know. But honestly? Let me know.

Sincerely,
Christina L. Barr

Did you know Phases of a Broken Sky is in the *Cursed Universe?*

Cursed Moon Series
Cursed Blood Series
Cursed Water Series

Enjoy this companion in the *Cursed Universe.*

Find out more: www.ninjadustpublishing.com

www.ingramcontent.com/pod-product-compliance
Lightning Source LLC
Chambersburg PA
CBHW050348030726
47503CB00008B/2680